SISTER STRONG

JAYLENE HALL

outskirtspress
DENVER, COLORADO

9/13

Outskirts Press, Inc.
http://www.outskirtspress.com

ISBN: 978-1-4787-0962-6

Outskirts Press and the "OP" logo are trademarks belonging to Outskirts Press, Inc.

PRINTED IN THE UNITED STATES OF AMERICA

Acknowledgments

I would like to thank first off, Paula Rudolph and family for helping me edit not only my first book, but also my second book before submission to the publishing company. She is such a wonderful lady! I would like to thank Megan Schmidt for being on the front cover with me representing "Macy". Then comes the acknowledgment to Kristy Hall with Kristy Hall Photography for taking the pictures for the cover of my dreams! The cover and author photo look absolutely amazing! I would also like to thank Scott Hall for answering all of my questions based on court set-ups. Thanks to all of my family and friends for supporting me not only with my first book, but also with my second book! I love you all! Thanks also to Janae for being a wonderful sister! And last but not least, thank-you God! You have blessed me with so much, and I will forever worship you!

With love,
Jaylene

Introduction

You never know what you have until it's gone. Love, for example. If you go around asking people what love means, they will probably say it's something you want forever or something you never want to let go of. If you ask them what the most important things they love in life are, it will probably be God, family, and friends.

Most people can't imagine their life without their family, or some just want a family. We all know, though we don't want to think about it, that things can happen in one second. In a blink of an eye, in a matter of time, bad things happen and we don't understand why. Why was it put on us to carry on with this pain?

My sister and I were best friends. Sometimes we didn't seem like it; other times you couldn't split us apart. She was such a big part in my life, such a big part no one could actually understand. I remember when I wanted a baby brother or sister so bad that I actually begged my parents for one. I remember the exact day my mom told me she was pregnant and the exact day she gave birth to my sister.

As she got older, I got to see her life play out. I used to run home after school to play with her when I was younger. Seeing her infant body made me think of a real life baby doll. I wanted to dress her, feed her, and play with her. We were six years apart; I couldn't do much with her until she got older.

As the years went by, things changed. We both got really busy, and we didn't see much of each other. It was my senior year, and she was only in sixth grade. I was too busy working out, practicing gymnastics, or hanging with my friends. She was the same way, so I only saw her maybe every other day in the morning or at gymnastics practice. I did get to see her if we ate supper together, but that didn't happen much because I just wanted to get fast food after sports practice.

She kept her focus on gymnastics, racing go-carts, and swimming. She was a great gymnast and traveled on the team with me, but she could also race a car at one hundred miles an hour and swim like a beast. I tried to come to most of her meets, but I didn't make all of them. She sure made me proud though, and I could have never asked for a better sister.

It is October 17, 2011, when I receive the worst phone call of my life. When I look at the caller ID, it says: Mom.

"Hello?" I answer.

"Hey, have you seen Lily at all today?" There is a bit of panic in her voice.

"Um…no…why?" I ask. At this moment I am working at our local movie theater downtown.

"Well, I was supposed to pick her up after school today, but when I got there, I waited for half an hour, and she never came out. I went into the school to look for her, and the office said that she hadn't signed out to leave early and that no one was looking for her until now. We called the bus barn, and the word got around to the drivers, but she wasn't riding on any buses at all. So I went home and waited. While I was waiting, I called all of her friends' parents and a few of her friends, and no one has seen her since school was over. She is not at any friends' houses either. So I called the cops, and they are on the lookout. They sent an investigator over to the school to see if there is any evidence there. So far there has been no sign of her. Your dad and I, along with the cops, are supposed to sit here at home and answer questions. It has been four hours! I'm seriously losing it; I'm scared. I'm worried sick! Where is she? I just...I'm so..." She starts to choke up and begins to cry.

"Mom, calm down...I'm coming home."

"No! Stay there in case she comes to look for you, because she knows you're at work, I told her this morning. Also... why haven't you answered your phone? I called you six times! I bought you that phone for a reason...this just makes matters worse!"

"Mom! Breathe! I'm at work and my phone was on silent...I'm sorry. I will stay here until my shift is over, and then I'm coming right home! Keep me posted!"

"OK...I love you!"

"Love you too!"

I hang up the phone, dizzy and confused. I try to think back this morning when I saw her last. She came into the bathroom while I was doing my hair. She looked like a zombie. Her hair was sticking up, and she was squinting her eyes. I had to giggle at her hair; I just couldn't help it.

"STOP IT!" she yelled at me.

"What?" I laughed.

"*About my hair!*" she yelled.

"Oh sorry, miss...*I'm in such a good mood!*" I joked with her.

She gave me a scowl and then hit me with her toothbrush.

"Yuck!" I screamed, and then I tackled her to the floor.

Mother came in and yelled at us for horsing around and told me I should leave soon before I was late. So I finished doing my hair, grabbed a banana, got in my truck, and started it up. Off to school I went.

I have a gut-wrenching feeling, almost like a chill to the bone, but I am burning with rage at the same time. How could my mom just let me stay at work when my sister has disappeared? I tell the manager and the workers about what has happened and to keep a lookout for her, in case she walks in. The manager tells me that I should take a rest and just sit down for a while. I tell him that I will keep working because it will keep my mind off of the subject.

I keep glancing at the clock...8:00...8:15...8:30...8:45... finally 9:00 p.m. My shift is over.

I grab my purse and leave. I get in my truck and fire up the engine. It is chilly out, being early fall. I am cold, but I don't turn up the heat because I want the chill to keep me awake. With my burning rage, I can't see straight. I have to breathe or else I will get in a tizzy fit.

By the time I reach the driveway, my heart leaps; four cop cars are sitting in the driveway. I am sure that when I walk in Lily will be sitting at the table, and this will all be a misunderstanding. Unfortunately I am wrong.

As I step inside, everyone turns and stares at me. My mother gets up from the dining room table and hugs me.

"Has anything happened?" I ask.

"No…we have given the cops Lily's paperwork and pictures. They are going through her Facebook and e-mail accounts, checking to see if there is any evidence there. They tried tracking her phone, but she must have turned it off or taken the battery out somehow."

"Okay…well, have you checked everywhere that she might be?" I ask.

"Yes, well, as far as I know. Some of the cops are still out searching."

"Okay…I have to sit down!" I say.

I sit down on one of the dining room chairs.

"If you don't mind…may we ask some questions?" one of the cops says. His badge says, *Officer Cane*.

"Yes, you may." I answer.

They ask me when I saw her last and how close our relationship is with each other. They ask me if she had seemed depressed lately or seemed to be edgy. They wonder if there are any secrets she had told me before, or if she seemed to act like she had some unspoken secrets.

I tell them that she didn't seem different, except a little more moody, because she was becoming a teenager and all. I knew that she was excited for fall, because she loves rolling down the hill in the leaves, and she loves carving pumpkins. She was getting amazing grades, and she was improving and moving up to another level of gymnastics. So right there, that tells you that she should be happy with her life. They tell me that since she is at the age of more stress, with school and friends, sometimes kids look up to other people for love or support—which can lead them into the arms of bad people.

I tell them that our family has always been close and that we tell each other everything. I always tell Lily that I love her, and so do my parents. We always say how we are so proud of her and what a wonderful person she is and will turn out to be.

They listen to me talk and take notes on their iPads. They are recording my every word, which makes me a bit nervous. When I finish up, they begin to do some talking themselves.

"It looks like you guys have a nice family here, but we can't let you off the hook so early. We still have to look around for evidence. Our team of investigators keep sending out messages, and so far we have found nothing."

At the same time, the walkie-talkie goes off: "Officer Cane, this is Officer Wellis, and we have found some evidence with team B at the school. We found a note in one of the recycling bins with what seems to have an old school paper of hers on the front and a few messages on the back."

"Ten-four, Officer Cane…what is on the note?"

"Just a few words to a friend. We are taking it down to the lab to check it out."

"Okay…I will inform the rest."

We all look at each other with questioning faces.

"Will they tell us what's on the note, officer?" my mom questions.

"Yes, but not until they have looked it over in the lab."

"Well…okay." I can tell my mom isn't in the mood to argue.

I look at the clock and it is already midnight. I think

maybe I should say something, but I figure it will make matters worse.

"It is getting awfully late, officer…what shall we do now?" my father asks.

"We will sit out in front of your house for a while…that way your family can have some alone time to talk or to get some sleep. We know this must be hard for you."

My mom nods as tears begin to build at the corner of her eyes. I have a hard lump forming in my throat. My ears have a horrible ringing inside them, and my chest becomes tight. My breakdown is coming; I can feel it. I try to hold my breath the best I can to keep from screaming. Once the cops say good-bye and that they would be right out front if we needed anything, I let the breath go. I let out a horrid scream that makes my mother and father jump. I get up from the chair, throw it into its place at the table, and run to my room. I slam the door and fall to the floor. I let the tears come; I let myself scream because for some reason I think that I will get my way. I will have her back and in my arms again, and this is only a nightmare. I take the book that is next to me and throw it across the room, hitting the picture of my sister and me at a restaurant for her birthday. I pick up the picture and look at it closely. Her eyes, her face, they just mesmerize me. How could a girl this precious to me be here one minute and gone the next?

I never get this worked up. This makes me go mad. Where is she and what happened? I am almost mad at her because maybe she wasn't paying attention. Girls can get kidnapped at an older age as well. They can be threatened by a weapon or forced. The thought scares me so much that I feel like I am going psycho. It is like I am an angry monster who wants to rip someone's face off.

I cry until my eyes are bloodshot, and my throat is tight. Finally I feel it…relief! Relief to relaxation! Have you ever cried so hard that when you take a deep breath, you slowly go to sleep? You know the saying, "I cried myself to sleep?" Well, I personally love the after-feeling of crying. It feels like I just let all of my emotions out, and I overworked my body. I can finally just relax and breathe. It's soothing to me; even though my makeup is dripping off my face and I can barely talk, it seems to calm me down.

I crawl to my bed and pray. I pray that God will bring her back to me, back to my arms…back to my welcoming arms. I curl up in my blankets and drift off to sleep.

Pain, Pain, Go Away...
I Don't Need You Anyway!

My headache is killing me. I wake up from my dreaded sleep; I hurt horribly. My back aches, which isn't uncommon for a gymnast. Also my throat is dry and hoarse. When I walk out into the living room, it is bare. I put on my coat and slippers and walk outside.

The cop car is gone and so are my parents. They must have taken my mom's car because it's gone. I walk back inside, slip into jogging pants and a sweatshirt, and I check on my sister in her room. When I walk into her room, I remember.

Her room is a mess, her bed isn't made, and her gym clothes are lying everywhere. Even though her room to any other person would look lived in, it now feels bare to me. It still feels like she should be home, asleep, snoring in her comfy bed. I would die to know where she is right now, what bed she is sleeping in, or even.... No! I can't think about her being dead, I just can't!

I turn away, not wanting to look at her room anymore. As I look at her gym clothes on the floor, it hits me! Yesterday at school she was supposed to have gym and she brings her gym clothes, even though she is only in sixth grade. She asked me if she could borrow my tennis shoes because hers were dirty. I gave her my Nike IDs; they are bright blue and pink and have my name on each tag, "Macy Hope." I watched her put them in her gym bag, and she took it to school with her. She never came home to give me them back! So she still has my shoes! That is one good piece of evidence the cops can use or look for.

I jump in my truck and speed off toward the police station, where I figure they must be.

———————

I open the door to the police station and walk up to the front desk.

"Hello there! What do you need?" a lady behind the front desk asks me. She is pale and has the messiest blonde hair. Her glasses are sliding off her face, and she has the saddest looking eyes. She looks like she hasn't slept in days.

"Um…hi…I'm Macy Hope and I was wondering if Ben Hope or Tamara Hope would be here by chance."

"Um…did they come in with Officer Cane?"

"Yup, that would be them," I reply.

"His office is down the hall and to the left," she says.

"Thank you," I reply as I begin to walk down the hall.

My parents are sitting in the office chairs as two officers are talking to them. I step inside, hoping not to make a big racket. They all look up and stare at me.

"Come sit," my mother replies and pats the chair next to her. "We were just talking about the lab overview."

Officer Cane and Officer Wellis explain to me that the note they had found had been no evidence at all; it only said random things and meant nothing. They tell me that they have searched the school and found a piece of evidence: a charm from her bracelet. They pull it out from a folder and show me through the little sandwich bag that it was put into.

"That was the charm I gave her for her birthday," I gasp. It's a heart with M&L on it; we got it specially engraved with the first letter of our names, reminding us of each other and sisterhood.

"Where did you find it?" I ask.

"We found it in the parking lot...a couple feet away from the playground. We figured that we would check it out in the lab since it has your sister's and your initials on it. Later, in the lab, we found her fingerprints on it but no one else's. We have not found the bracelet or any other charms...yet," Officer Wellis says.

"Well...okay." I didn't know what to say, so I stayed quiet the whole time.

On the way home it's dreadful. It's cloudy out and it begins to rain. I walk inside and sit on the couch, looking out the window. The forest out back is calming. The forest is my happy place; it makes me feel relaxed and alive. In a way I almost feel as if I am in heaven out there, with the way it looks and smells, and the noise it makes when the breeze rushes through the trees. There is a creek that runs in the middle of the forest and a tree that has fallen over it, which fits perfectly from the edge of the timber to all across the creek. It's like walking across a bridge. Sometimes things in nature seem impossible, like how could that tree exactly fit from the end of the timber all the way to the exact end of the creek? Maybe God planned it to grow that tall, so when it fell it would make a bridge just for me. When I was younger, I would go out there and enjoy what felt like the world of nature. It made me appreciate life and how much it meant to me. Now when I look out across there, I feel peace, though it still haunts me to think, *Does Lily have peace right now?*

I don't understand how God could give me something so precious and then take it away from me. It's like a cold game of hide and seek: "I'll hide her...you come find her!" But I can't think that way. God will help me through this, I tell myself. He will help me through this.

My mom is downstairs sitting at her desk, staring off into space.

"You okay, Mom?" I ask as I creep down the stairs.

"Um...yeah...well, no...well, I was just drinking some coffee," she replies.

"Oh...Mom, you know... if you want to talk..."

She shakes her head and a tear begins to fall down her cheek. She blinks her blue eyes and then shuts them tight.

"Mom..." I mumble.

"I...have...a headache," she mumbles back.

I watch her cry for a while; I try to comfort her. She says she needs her space, her time alone. I leave and I get on Facebook; a million people have posted, asking me, "Are you okay?" or "I'm so sorry about what happened!" or "Have you found out anything?"

I shut the computer down. I can't read them, not now anyway. It hurts to see people posting to me! It felt normal posting on other people's profiles like that but not having them post on my own. No, I can't stand it.

I start the hot bathwater and sink slowly into the tub. The warm water is heaven. I let out a sigh and then a tear trickles into the water. Then more flow down my cheek. How I wish I could cry on someone's shoulder or scream at someone just to let my built-up anger out. I could call my friends back since they have left me fifty messages already in my in-box and on voice mail, but I just ignore them. They should understand; I need time to make this reality. To realize it before I can talk about it.

I let myself cry. I cry through my bath, cry through the songs I listen to, and cry through the night. All night I cry, scream, kick, shake, and tremble. The thoughts won't stop spinning in my head: *"Where is she? What is she doing? Is she alive? Is she being abused?"*

I can't stand it! The pain I feel now is the worst pain I have ever felt. It's not physical pain, it's emotional pain. I feel like the pain I am tortured with now…is only the beginning.

My Letter to You~

Dear Lily,

It's Halloween today. I know it's one of your favorite seasons. I carved a pumpkin with a heart and your name on it. It feels like forever since I have talked to you, but really it has only been a week. I hope you're safe. If you get this, can you write me back? You would know our address, right? Ha-ha! Hey, I miss you! If you get this, can you please come home? We all want you back into our loving arms. Love you!

Love,
Your sister, Macy :)

I tie the letter to the string of the pink balloon. I decide that since I can't talk to her at this moment, I will send a balloon into the sky with a note to her attached to it. The good thing is I will not know where it goes so I can maybe have some hope that she is out there somewhere. Maybe she will see it in the sky, or maybe it will remind her of home with its pink color, our favorite color. Maybe she will think of me! Though I doubt it will happen that way because the balloon can float anywhere. It will probably pop when it gets high enough in the air with all of the pressure. I am still going to do it anyway because it makes me feel better. It gives me a little more reassurance within myself if I can somehow talk or write to her in a physical form.

I take a deep breath, and then I send it free. I watch it float to the sky, the breathless air sweeping it away. The balloon's tender touch as I release the grip of my hand, is like her heart. I let out a sigh and then turn back on my heels and crunch through the leaves.

I feel my phone vibrate in my pocket. The caller ID says, "Chelsea, New Text Message."

Chelsea: Hey, whatcha doing 2nite?

Me: Idk...y?

Chelsea: Want 2 go 2 the movie *Soul Surfer* 2nite, and maybe out 4 pizza and shakes?

Me: Idk...

Chelsea: Come on! It will be me, Brett, Lena, West, and Blake.

Me: Sounds like fun but idk...

Chelsea: Really? U haven't been the same since...well... u know...and u haven't had a lot of fun lately so y not come hang with us and get the stress off your mind!

Me:	Sighhhhh…ur kinda rite
Chelsea:	Ya girly…IK!
Me:	K…what time?
Chelsea:	5:30…in 30 minutes ;)
Me:	K…Ill meet u at the theater.
Chelsea:	Yo! Cheer up…West is gonna be there ;)
Me:	So over him…
Chelsea:	Since when??
Me:	Since…I havent seen u in like 4eva! Lol tell ya later
Chelsea:	That's the spirit! Finally got an lol in there ;) cya there

I walk up to the house and through the door, feeling my whole body defrost from the house's warmth. October is getting a little chilly! I look in the mirror; I have no makeup on and my hair is a mess! I grab my curling iron and put some curls in my hair. I throw on some mascara, apply blush on my washed-out face, and smear on some lip gloss. I grab my skinny jeans and put them on along with my Rue 21 long-sleeved shirt, and I slip on my brown Uggs. It feels good to dress up again. Ever since she has disappeared I haven't felt like doing anything with myself.

With my purse by my side, I drive down the driveway in my truck.

I pull into the parking lot. As I am getting out of my truck, I step on something. I roll my ankle and trip, making a fool of myself. I look down to see what I had tripped on. It's a shoe, a Nike shoe. Smashed from being run over. It looks familiar to me, almost too familiar. Wait...I look on the tag in the front. They are a pair of expensive IDs; they are my Nike IDs that Lily had before...she...disappeared!

Ha, Gotcha! I'm One Clue Closer to You!

I am surrounded by everyone: cops, my family, and friends. All right there in the movie theater parking lot. Using plastic gloves, the cops gently lift the shoe into the bag and seal it…tight!

Lena puts her arms around me, and West holds my hand. They all reassure me that it will be OK, but somehow I know differently.

The look on my parents' faces disturb me; I shall never see that look again. It frightens me to the bone, it breaks my heart, it makes me realize that life is hard, and so is love.

I turn away after answering all the questions that I can. I answered cops, reporters, my friends, and my parents. That was enough. I walk into the theater with my friends trailing behind me. They know not to ask if I still feel like seeing the movie. They know that I need to get away from all of this, even if I am only inside the door from all the commotion outside.

———◦———

The movie got me thinking. That girl, Bethany, is so

strong—not only physically, but mentally. She didn't stop reaching her dreams; she pushed herself until she succeeded. Just because she only had one arm didn't mean that she only had one percent of confidence…she had one hundred percent. Something hit! Something…someone…somehow it came to me. Maybe it came from God himself. I knew right then and there that she wasn't gone forever. She is out there somewhere! She isn't dead; she could very well be suffering, but she won't give up! It is my job to find her! Yet I have no idea how…but I am going to find her! I am going to be strong!

———◦◦◦———

"Are you sure you want to do this?" Chelsea asks me.

"Chelsea…don't doubt me; I will get it!" I reply.

"I'm not doubting you…I'm just assuring you."

The police have Lily's laptop at the moment, so I am doing my own investigating. I have every laptop I own scattered around my desk. One opened with Facebook, one with e-mail, one with Nike's home page, and one with the worldwide news home page. I know all of her passwords, because she uses the same one for everything. I take notes:

- *Facebook: Check all of Lily's friends, all of their latest updates and pictures posted. Check my Facebook, and all of my friend's latest posts and pictures.*
- *Nike: Check insurance on tennis shoes for IDs; see if they can be on the lookout for my shoes.*
- *E-mail: Who e-mailed her last, and who is on her e-mail list of contacts, all of her e-mails ever sent?*

- *World Wide News: Any reports about her or me?*

The reason why I am hacking all of her profiles is to see if I can find something that the cops can't. I know her better than they do, and if I can sense something wrong, I'll make sure to figure out what's causing it!

I look for what feels like forever! Chelsea checks all of the Nike pages and news reports, and I check the Facebook and e-mail accounts.

3:55 p.m. "Found anything yet?" I ask Chelsea.

"Nope," she replies.

4:55 p.m. "Chelsea! I think I have found something!"

"What! What is it?" she asks anxiously.

I open up her friend's "Frappiero Reneaz's" profile. "His last post was posted on the day she went missing," I explain to her. His post said, "Finally, I have gotten this far. I shall not look back but to keep running!"

"It was posted at almost 8:00 p.m., which would be during the time she went missing!" I explain.

"Why did she 'friend' this guy anyway? Do you know him?" she asks me.

"I have never seen him or heard of him," I reply.

"Look under his picture!"

I open up his entire list of pictures. He is a tall, pale, brunet. He has a mole on his forehead and the style of a gangster. In most of the pictures, he has a gangster hat on and a sweatshirt. He is not cute…at all!

"What a weirdo!" Chelsea says.

"He seems too suspicious to me! I'm going to print out his Facebook page and give it to the cops," I say.

"Wait! No, what you also need to do is set up a new Facebook account with a picture of a really pretty girl on it and make up a different name…and then you friend him!" Chelsea replies.

"O-M-G! Chelsea, that is why you are my best friend!" I laugh. We give each other a high five. Ten minutes later I have a new Facebook account under "Tera Lee." I took a picture of a random girl off the Internet and put it on "Tera's" profile. I send the friend request and log off Facebook.

"So what did you find out about the Nike insurance?" I ask Chelsea.

"I really have no idea; how about we just deal with the Facebook problem for now and leave the rest for the cops, or for later," she replies.

"That sounds good."

The more I think about it, the more I wonder if I am jumping a little too fast. The cops have my back, so all I have to do is print out all of the copies and hand them over. How hard can that be? I just need time to relax.

"Want to grab a latte?" Chelsea asks.

"Sounds great…I need one." I sigh. For the first time, I laugh a little. Maybe being one step closer to solving a mystery makes me feel a little more at ease. But still, deep down in there, I feel a burning ring of fire: hatred.

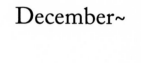

December~

A Winter without You

I walk into gymnastics for the first time since her disappearance. Walking in, it smells like chalk, sweat, and what used to be pretty much my home. I was at the gym more of the time than my actual home. Working out was me. Before she went missing, that's all I would do—workout, eat, sleep, and go to school. Gymnastics was my sport. I loved the feeling of flipping in the air, and bending and twisting in impossible directions that most people would break their back doing. I could do every split down to the floor, have my legs go over my head, and have every muscle pop out. It was my ambition, my hobby. Working out was my way of relieving stress; it calmed me down, kept me in tune.

I started working out at age ten after I realized that I didn't feel comfortable in my body. I was growing, but I still had some extra chub on me. So I bought an iPod and started walking every night, and I mean *every* night. After about a month or so, I was showing some pretty good results. I was thinning out. So I decided to kick it up a notch; I turned the walking into jogging. By the time I

JAYLENE HALL

did that I looked good but not great…yet! I was so happy about losing the extra chub that I didn't notice that I was slowly building muscle. That summer I started running three miles a night with my dad. Then I also added some reps of sit-ups, push-ups, and muscle work. That's when I got excited. That summer I worked out almost every day for two hours of hard, hard ab work and legwork. I felt and looked great.

I then started gymnastics at the end of sixth grade. They put me on the team, and I started working out even more. I went there three days a week for four hours each. I loved it! I got hooked. I was learning so much by challenging my body and myself. Some things felt impossible, yet I worked my tail off. I still worked out at home and kept up with my grades. I was a busy girl!

Gymnastics is about challenging your body, and how hard our bodies can work and bend! Gymnastics shows flexibility and confidence. I love every minute of it.

As I open the gym door, my coach, Renea, is there to greet me.

She gives me a hug and apologizes about my sister. I thank her and tell her how much I appreciate it.

"It's been a while since I have seen you at the gym," she jokes.

"I know! It's good to be back!" I reply.

"You sure you want practice tonight?" she asks.

"Yes, I need this and so does my body!" I laugh.

"Well, go in and stretch well; it's been about three months."

"Will do! I'll do some stunts on the trampoline too," I say and laugh.

Gymnastics is a skill of flexibility and strength, and once your body gets used to it, it's hard to stop.

After being out for almost three months without even working out, my body has been killing me. Some people might think I am crazy, but I hurt more when I don't work out than I do if I am sore from an extreme workout.

After some hugs from my old gym pals, I make it to the tumble track. I run and start with a simple front tuck, easy. Then I go for a front layout onto the big, squishy mat at the end. I flip, straight as a stick, and I stick it! For some odd reason this surprises me, but it shouldn't because I have stuck them many times. After doing several more, landing them, and sticking them, my coach comes over to me.

"Now do a front full," Renea says.

"Oh, I don't know. It has been a while!" I sigh.

"I know that, ha-ha-ha, but I also know that you can do one as well!" she chuckles.

"Um…you sure?" I half chuckle, half cringe.

"Come on! I will spot you on one." she says.

"Um…okay." I sigh. I am not sure if she can or how she can spot me on a front full, but like every gymnast has to do, we have to trust that our coaches won't let us drop or fall. If they do, likely they will cushion the landing for you. So I walk to the end of the long, narrow tumble track, take a deep breath, and run toward her. I pump my legs, and with each step, I push off of the trampoline. Closer and closer! Finally I hit the end, the blue strip, and fly up into the air. I feel her arms gently grab my hips as she tries to toss me up high and out. I tuck my arms in and keep my body tight. I really can't see anything until my last half. I bend my knees and stay as still as possible. Amazingly, I completely stick it! I look over at her.

"See!" she says as she gives me a pat on the back. "Well done!"

Then right after she says that, I do something that I haven't done in a while…I actually smile! Somehow it feels like a stranger to me, like I never have smiled before. Like it's something that I have only seen, not done! I haven't seen anyone smiling in my house for a while. Everyone is so caught up in their own little world. I guess I am too. I used to smile all the time, when I felt good at least. I thought it felt good to smile; it made me feel happy, but after she disappeared it seemed like when I wanted to smile, I wanted to get sick. It disgusted me, I guess. Maybe it's a good thing that I came back to the gym, I actually feel happy here.

"All right, Macy, go to vault," Renea tells me.

Vault was my best event at competitions. It was also one of my favorites, along with floor.

"All right, Macy, I want you to do a front handspring off the table to warm up, okay?"

"Okay, sounds good," I reply.

I start at my certain number that I am set to run from, and I salute. I look the table straight in the eye, and I run right for it. My front handspring is iffy. It's a little bit sideways and loose. I knew my first one wouldn't be the best, but I try and try again. I do eight front handsprings all together until she tells me to move on to gangers. I look at her like she is crazy. *You expect me to do what?* I think to myself.

"Um…I don't know if I'm ready for that…it *has* been a while," I tell her.

"Macy, I have seen you do many, and so I believe you can do them!" she replies.

I swear, I think she is crazy! I have been gone for three months and now she wants me to do gangers over the table? I am really thinking something bad is going to happen, but, hey, what could go worse?

"Macy, come on. I will spot you into the foam pit!"

I breathe a heavy sigh. "All right…I guess."

"There is no I guess, Macy," she says, "you will!"

"Okay," I reply. I go to my starting number, salute, and I sprint to the vault. I'm a little shy about hitting the springboard, but I do. I do a roundoff from the vault, and I try to do a back tuck right from it, but my force becomes weak and I fall right on my head. I was too low to even attempt a flip anyway.

I get up with a struggle, a little dizziness left in me. Renea helps me to my feet.

"Try again, but this time shoot higher up and out," she tells me.

I try again and again and again. Each of the five times I land on my head. On the last one my neck pops out, and I start to get frustrated. I let hot tears prickle down my cheek. Renea must have noticed because she wipes my tears away.

"Look at me," she says. "You have to get aggressive with this!"

I nod.

"Nothing comes easy in gymnastics unless you push yourself to make it. I know life has been hard on you, probably harder than I understand, but this is why you are here, Macy! I can let you sit around and pout, or I can make you pick yourself up and push yourself to become who you used to be! Right now, all that anger has built up in you, and I can see it. In your eyes there is worry, fear, and anger. You have to release that energy somehow…don't you? Have you worked out at all these last three months?"

"No, I have been too busy dealing with my sister's mess and my grades at school," I reply.

"Exactly! So you have all that anger and frustration built up in your body, and it wants to get out. So right now is your chance. I want you to work so hard that you cry. Scream at me, run at the vault, flip through the air, and push so hard your muscles start to give out! Got me?"

"Yes," I reply, soaking in what she just said.

"Um…I said scream at me! Not shy away from me!" she yells.

"I said *fine*!" I yell at her.

"There!" she laughs. "That's what I want to hear."

We both laugh. I start at my starting number, salute, and then take a deep breath. I lunge forward, thinking to myself, *Why did you take her away from me? Why didn't she say goodbye? How could this have happened to me? Why does life have to be so hard? How can I live with this pain?*

All of the anger shoots out of me as I pick up the pace. I run as fast as my body will let me. I am running so hard that it feels like I am outrunning myself. I can't stop. By the time I hit the springboard, I am shot up into the air. My hands lightly pound off the table. I quickly tuck my legs to my chest and feel my body fight gravity. I am flying. My body over-rotates backward, and I am left to the solid ground. My feet land, and my body is tight and withheld, while my inner conscience is bursting. I stand up and actually laugh. I look at Renea who is shaking her head.

"See," she says, "sometimes all you need is a little boost!"

The First Snowfall

By the time we move on to the bars, my hands are on fire. I receive a blood blister on my left hand and a rip on the right. I am still able to do my giants, but I have to practice being tight. It feels good to be on bars again. My dismounts go quite well until I over-rotate out of one of my double backs and land on my back. Being a senior and all, it is hard to do gymnastics with a body that's fully mature, and it's hard to be light on your feet with the amount of weight and height.

Renea moves me on to conditioning after bars. Conditioning is like working out with sit-ups, push-ups, etc., and my body is worn out by the time we are finished.

<hr/>

I have just put on my jogging pants and begin to walk out of the gym, when I think of you. The cold hits my body like a sudden heart attack as I open the door. I walk outside into the winter air. I see it…snow! It sprinkles the ground like a bunch of cotton balls thinned out. Of course I have seen snow before, many times, but this time it catches me off guard. It makes me think of you.

The first snowfall of last year, you woke me up from my sleep.

"Macy…Macy…MACY! Wake up, wake up, wake up!" Lily chanted.

I slightly groaned; she was getting annoying.

"What?" I finally answered, after I was able to comprehend her from my daze.

"The snow! The snow! It's the first snowfall; come on!" she replied as she dragged me out of bed and made me step out onto our wet, snowy deck. I let out a muffled laugh.

"Wow, for the first snowfall, it is actually pretty," I mumbled.

"So guess what that means!" she said.

"Um…what?" I replied, kind of puzzled. "Our tradition, remember?" she said.

"Oh yes, how could I forget!" I laughed.

Every snowfall my family has a tradition we follow. No matter how cold it is or how much snow there is, we have to go outside and walk in the storm. If there is enough snow, we collect it, take it inside, and make homemade ice cream with it. Then we have hot chocolate from either Starbucks or from our homemade recipe.

That year, there was enough snow on the ground to make homemade ice cream for each other. We sat around the fireplace on a cold Saturday, and we played a game of Candyland. I can still see her face, all lit up and happy, like a sparkling angel. I will never forget that.

As I hop in the car, my mom looks at me.

"How was practice?" she asks, our usual conversation.

"It went well. I'm still a little bit rusty, but I will have to get back in sync with it all, I guess," I reply.

"Well, that's good to hear." She is quiet for a while.

"The snow is pretty," she finally speaks.

"Um…yeah," I reply, feeling a little bit of uneasiness. I haven't spoken to my mother in a while. She seems so distant. Every word that comes out of her mouth is negative. She doesn't want to talk about Lily or me. She just wants to nitpick about every single thing that goes wrong. After a while I stopped listening to her, and she got the hint, so we quit talking to one another. My dad, on the other hand, is using work to get his mind off the stress. I don't see him much anymore, nor do I talk to him either. I guess we are all trapped in our own little worlds. My mom doesn't even cook supper anymore, but she has become a neat freak. She scrubs the floors every day on her bare hands and knees. Her knees are raw from the chemicals, and her hands are dry from the soap. She vacuums three times a day, and if my room has one shirt lying out, she makes me wash it with my bare hands. Though she does not raise her voice, she puts her anger into her scrubbing utensils and gets to work. I make supper most of the time for my dad and me. I have become a pretty good cook, but my mother won't eat what I make. My dad argues with her to become realistic about this, that she is losing it. She rudely tells him to shut his mouth, and then she gets back to work. My dad does not go any further with the conversation. He leaves her at peace.

As we pull in the drive, I get out and walk inside. I think I would have felt better if I just drove myself home from gymnastics, but my truck is at the detailing shop getting detailed. I have saved up my money to have it get a nice cleaning. My truck deserves it, and sometimes I think I do too. I grab an apple, do my homework, and then, as I am sitting down at my desk, I hear a ding from my computer. I open it up and realize that Frappiero Reneaz has just accepted me as a friend on Facebook. I literally about fall out of my seat. It has been a whole month since I sent him a friend request, and now he has finally accepted it! I call Chelsea right away.

"Chelsea, it finally happened; he responded!"

"Wait, what? You mean he responded to your friend request?" she asks eagerly.

"Yes, Chelsea, he responded just two minutes ago!"

"O-M-G! Has he sent you a message or anything?"

"Um...no, but I can check to see if he is on chat!"

"Okay...hurry!"

"No luck, he friended me from his phone so I don't think he is on anymore," I reply. "Wait, Chelsea! He has his phone! The cops can track him down!"

"Oh yeah! Okay, print off his Facebook info, along with some pictures of him, and take it to the station!" she yells.

"But what if it is a set up?" I cry.

"Doesn't matter. Would you rather be one step closer or one step behind the evidence?" she asks.

"Um...one step closer," I say.

"Exactly. Do it now before he turns off his phone or something!" she yells.

"Okay, I have to go. Bye!" I say.

"Call me when you get more details," she says as she hangs up.

———— ◆ ————

"Okay, here is the printed off version of his profile and some of his pictures," I say as I hand all of the info to Officer Cane.

"And I should look at this because?" he asks.

"Because it is a part of evidence…maybe," I say.

I explain to him about how I found him on Lily's Facebook page and about what he posted on the night she went missing. I also explain how I made a fake profile page of a girl named Tera Lee. I friended him, and he responded a month later with his phone.

My parents are looking at me like I am crazy; it is 11 o'clock at night and I am wasting their time. Officer Cane, though, seems to be astounded.

"Wow, smart girl you have here," he tells my parents. I gently smile and say a thank-you.

"Um…it is clear that you do have some evidence toward him, but we will need more. So before you jump off your stool, the other officers and I need to research and look up more about him," he explains.

My parents both give me a soft smile.

"So go home, get some sleep, and I will give you guys a call if we happen to find out anything more," he says.

"Will do!" I reply as I get up and turn the corner. I ignore my parents' faces the whole time. They probably think I am crazy, but I sure know where this is going. They aren't going to stop me. I'm one step closer to hearing her scream my name. I can hear her a million miles away.

To Live, Laugh, and Love without You

I'm so sore that I can't move one muscle in my body without screaming in pain. So much for jumping right into stunts I haven't done for three months at gymnastics.

The ground is covered in snow, about three inches from the heavy snowfall overnight. The sun has not peeked out at all. I'm going to go sledding with Chelsea, Blake, and West. I have not had a lot of time for friends lately, except at school. Today is Saturday, and I have some free time.

———◆———

It is cold and I can barely feel my hands. West insists that I wear his gloves, but his hands are twice as big as mine. He only laughs when I put them on. Chelsea and Blake are officially "boyfriend and girlfriend." I feel bad; I'm a senior, but I have never actually had what seems like a serious boyfriend. I have dated guys, yes, but I'm not too interested in them. Except West, he is…well…different. He is the captain of the football team and has a cute face and smile, but he is not a stuck-up jerk. He can actually carry on a conversation with people without showing his ego. He seems like my type: sweet, nice, and true to himself.

"You're crazy!" he says as he throws a snowball at me.

"Excuse me!" I say as I am in the middle of building a snowball, feeling the urge to laugh.

"You heard me! You are crazy because you wear thin gloves on a freezing winter day!" he says and laughs.

"Well, I was in a hurry, OK?" I yell as I start laughing. Chelsea and Blake are laughing as well.

"You guys need to ride the sled down the hill together while Blake and I race you," says Chelsea.

"Like little kids?" I ask.

"Um, excuse me? You are one," she tells me as she laughs.

"Ohhh…good one!" I say.

West is sitting behind me. He wraps his arms around me and tells me to hold on. An instant rush hits my body as we fly down the hill—the biggest and most dangerous hill in the park, I must add. More than six kids have been hurt going down this thing, but that's what makes it so fun.

I am screaming so loud but laughing at the same time. I can hear West laughing in my ear. The breeze feels good on my face, and I feel as if I am flying until we skid to a stop. Not even two feet behind us are Chelsea and Blake, heading right for our sled. West lets out a sudden scream, and the next minute I am thrown overboard. My body hits the ground like a rock, and I feel my whole back pop out of place, but I can't stop laughing. I am laughing so hard that I am crying.

West was thrown a few feet beside me, and Chelsea and

Blake are spread out on our sled. They are all screaming with laughter. I swear the neighbors around us can hear us for miles, but we don't care. We are just teenagers being stupid, which makes it even more laughable.

West helps me up and carries me all the way back to my truck; we throw our sleds into the back and hop in to defrost our frozen fingers and toes. We then head off for Starbucks.

Sipping my hot chocolate that West gladly bought for me, I am sitting in a booth with my three friends, saying over and over what a wonderful adventure that we are having today.

"How is it," West asks, "that you can be so calm even though your sister is missing? How do you still find happiness?"

"Well…I guess that one might seem calm on the outside but maybe not always in the inside. There have been many nights that I just wanted to scream at the world, but there is a part of me that tells me that she is out there waiting for me. Some nights I can hear her in my dreams telling me that she is OK. I don't always know what exactly that means, as for dead or alive, but I know she's out there. I picture her telling me that I will be OK and that I can stay strong no matter what. I guess what I have is faith," I tell him as Chelsea pats me on the back.

"You are strong, Mac (my nickname from her.) No doubt about it." she says.

"You know, guys, today has been the first day that I have actually laughed in a while," I say.

"Maybe today is telling you something," Chelsea says.

I instantly think about it…moving on. It has been three

months, long and stressful at that. It was time to laugh, to smile, and to cheer again. Even if she's gone doesn't mean I'm gone. I will put up a fight to find her, to hold her again, but I will not stand around and pout in a corner for that day to come. I will stay strong and courageous like it says in Joshua 1:9.

The day that she left me...I shall use my laughs and smiles as much as I can, because just like my sister, any day could be your last.

To Track You Down

Today is Monday. Dreadful Mondays drain my spirits. As though the fun of yesterday feels like a wave of good-bye today. I am walking down the hallway, computer case in my hand, with math and science textbooks, and a cup of coffee from Starbucks. I sit in my first science class of the day with much to learn. My teacher gently hands out our reports that were checked from a week ago. Mine has a nice *A+* on it.

Chelsea meets me in the hall at noon.

"Yo, Mace, do you got practice tonight, eh?" she asks.

"First of all, I don't think the French use 'yo,' and you need to learn to roll your tongue more on 'practice,' eh?" I quote.

"Yo, shut it; I'm slowly getting French down, okay!" she remarks.

"Ha-ha-ha…yup, you got a lot to learn!" I joke. She laughs and then punches me in the arm.

"Girl, what happened to your big buffy arms?" she asks.

"Hadn't been to the gym until last week and the stress ate it away."

"Well, how about you and I hit the gym tonight...you know, jus' youwah and moowah!" she jokes.

"Yeah, your French sucks and so do my arms, so it sounds like a deal!" I say.

"Ha-ha-ha, okay, sounds good!" She gives me a wink and then we walk on to lunch.

———— ◦◉◦ ————

"Hey, turn up the stereo!" Chelsea yells across the fitness room. "Brokenhearted" from Karmin blasts over the speakers. I sit down on the bench for arm presses and stack it up to fifty. I then start doing the reps while Chelsea is at the ab cruncher.

"You know what?" she asks me between breaths.

"What?" I ask as I take it to sixty.

"Blake was talking to that blond chick during fourth period today. Should I be worried?" she asks.

"Nah, maybe he just needed some homework help or something."

"I don't know..." she responds.

"Look..." I say as I pick it up to seventy-five, "just let it go until you see them together again, and then ask him about it."

"Okay. Hey, have you heard any more about the Frappiero Reneaz?" she asks.

"No. I sent the evidence to the cops and so far I haven't heard anything back," I say.

"Maybe you should keep checking your Facebook in case he gets on chat," she says.

"Yeah, I'll check when I get home," I reply. I move on to leg lifts.

"You ready for college?" she asks me.

"Yeah, I think I'm going to college for fine arts," I reply.

"Nice. I'm going for nursing," she says.

"You would make a great nurse; just don't use your French to impress the doctors because you might just scare them a little," I joke.

"Ha ha, you're funny!" she smirks. I look out the door and there is West watching me do leg lifts.

"Hey!" I jog over to him.

"Didn't feel like working out today?" I joke as I give him a little punch.

"Um, no, basketball practice kind of got me tired today!" he chuckles.

I'm not a basketball player. Neither is Chelsea. So that's one thing we have in common.

"So how long have you been working out?" he asks.

"Little less than an hour," I reply as he tucks a piece of loose hair behind my ear. I blush slightly.

"Well…have fun!" he laughs.

"When is working out not fun!" I wink as I walk back to the bench.

"Ha, see ya," he says as he walks away smiling. Chelsea gives me a flirty look.

"Oh, stop it!" I laugh as I start blushing.

"You two would make a hot couple," she jokes. I laugh and then throw my sweat towel at her.

"Yuck!" she screeches.

I laugh as I put my shoes on, ready to go.

"Hey," she says as she gives me a sweaty hug, "I'm glad you're back to your happy self." I smile to myself.

"You know what? I'm glad too," I say.

When I get home, I check my Facebook. I start out with all of my notifications, and then I check all of the news feed. I glance over at the chat, and suddenly my heart starts racing. Frappiero Reneaz is on chat!

"Mom! MOM!!" I start screaming as I run out into the hall and down the stairs, slipping on the wet hardwood floor.

"Mommmm!" I yell as I run into her by the office door.

"What is it, honey?" she asks.

"He is on chat…*he is on*!!"

It takes her no time to run up the stairs behind me into my room and to my computer.

"What do I do?" I ask.

"Um…send him a chat message," she replies.

"What do I say?"

"Um…tell him something about how you think he is cute or something!" she says.

"What! Have you seen his face?" I remark.

"Just do it; he can give us more clues," she says. I send him a chat:

Tera Lee (me):	Hey, I think you're really cute! Just thought I would tell ya! ;)
Frappiero Reneaz:	Oh…why, thank you! You are pretty yourself.
Tera Lee:	Thanks…where do u live? Maybe we could meet up sometime!?

Frappiero Reneaz: Well, right now I am kind of touring places.

Tera Lee: Like where? :)

Frappiero Reneaz: Well, right now I am touring New York.

Tera Lee: Oh...fun! Where in New York?

Frappiero Reneaz: Um...that's kind of personal information.

Tera: Yeah...right lol. Don't want to be no stalker or anything...ha-ha-ha! Frappiero Reneaz is off line.

"Okay, Mom. He is somewhere in New York," I say.

"I will have the cops use an Internet scanner to see where his chat messages are coming in from," she replies as she is talking to an officer on the phone.

"I want you to print out what you just chatted him and keep all of the time records together," she also tells me.

I run it off the printer and then put the papers in with the info about him. Mother drives me to the station.

The cops take a whole hour looking over the evidence, finding his hot-spot location, and trying to key up on all of his background. Apparently, they cannot track him down by his phone (must be discontinued), but they do find the location where he was when he was using the Internet server. He is in New York City.

"Well, what we can do is send some undercover policemen to track him down and take him in for questioning. If that makes you feel more comfortable."

"Comfortable! Are you kidding me? This isn't a game of

Duck Duck Goose…who finds who! He has my sister!" I yell. "You can't ask my family if it would make us more comfortable just to go track down a kidnapper…he is a stranger who has an innocent child, for crying out loud!"

The lady looks taken back.

"Well, we aren't sure that he has your sister, but yes, we will have them track him down," she mumbles.

"Well, good, because even if he didn't kidnap my sister, he could still very well be some crazy man who kidnapped someone else's kid," I reply.

"Now, honey, just calm down," my mother tells me.

"Nothing is ever going to calm this family down until we find her!" I yell.

On the Run

Mother comes in with a bowl of hot chili. It's the first time she has cooked in a while.

"They sent the undercover cops out today to New York," she tells me. "They said that they will keep us posted with e-mails and calls. They are still having the investigators investigate the school and the town back here, but I doubt if they will find anything," she says.

"I wouldn't doubt it," I tell her. "Who would have thought that I would find my Nike ID shoe that she had in the movie theater's parking lot?"

"True, but why the movie theater?" she asks.

"I don't know…maybe for a setup or cover-up," I tell her.

"Well, tonight is Tuesday and you have gymnastics, so you better go," she says as she gets up. I still have homework to do from school today, so I pack up my books and head out to the truck. Sometimes our coaches let us do homework while we are at practice.

"Warm up, girls!" our coach, Renea, yells.

I do ten laps around the floor and then some front tucks, double tucks, and roundoff backhand springs. I then stretch my splits and head off to my first event: floor.

"Today, Macy, I want you working double gangers into the foam pit."

For some of you who don't know, that's when you jump, twist to your back, and do two back flips in the air before you land.

"Okay," I reply before I salute. I stare at the floorboard, ready to bounce into motion. I instantly sprint down the floor and rebound my feet at the edge. My body throws itself up and out as I finish my last tuck. It all happens so fast.

"Well done," Renea tells me. "Five more just like that, but a little faster and tighter next time."

Time passes, and I move on to bars and then to conditioning. She has us do thirty pull-ups all together, seventy-five push-ups, 150 sit-ups, twenty leg lifts, and ten minutes worth of running. I am truly tired by the end of practice.

As I get in the car, I check my phone and see that I have a text. It's from West.

West: Are you done with practice?

Me: Yeah…you?

West: Do you want to hang out?

Me: Sure…but what would we do, it's almost nine.

West: We could get a smoothie at the Shake Shack ☺

Me: OK ☺

Nine o'clock at the shake shack:

"So you ready for graduation?" West asks.

"Ha ha, yeah, I'm kind of afraid to leave my parents though; they might be kind of lost. I'm the only one it seems who is keeping my family together."

"Oh, I'm sorry," he says. I sip my smoothie.

"Oh, it's okay. I'll find her and bring her home," I say.

"I know you will. I have faith in you Macy," he tells me.

"Well, thank you," I say.

My phone starts to ring. It's Mom.

"Honey, HONEY! You need to come home!" she says.

"Why, what's wrong?" I ask.

"They found her fingerprint in New York City!"

"What? I'll be right there!" I say as I get up to leave.

"West, I'm so sorry but it's about my sister…I have to leave," I tell him.

"No, I get it…go quickly!" he says as he gives me a quick, soft hug.

———⊙———

I sit down at the table in the police station. The cop explains to us that they have found a fingerprint on one of the shelves, close to where a video game on clearance was stolen. They also found video footage of her stealing the video game, but she was gone before the cops could track her down.

"Wait…Lily stealing? I doubt it," I say.

"But she could be being forced or harassed by someone, like the kidnapper, to steal the stuff!" the cop replies.

"Are they still tracking her down?" I ask.

"Yes, of course; we sent out more investigators and search warrants, along with a search party," the cop explains.

"So she is definitely alive?" I ask.

"Well, at that point she was, so hopefully she is still alive," the cop says.

"Okay, well, hopefully you are trying your hardest to find her so I can see her in person and not under a video camera. And if I find out that you and your people are slacking off on your job I will…"

"Macy! Just go home; you have said enough," my mother tells me.

I get in my truck and slam the door.

I make my decision at that point: if they can only dig so far for evidence, I will take my own darn shovel and dig down to the source myself!

Christmas Break without You

"Mom, I have made up my mind," I tell her.

"With what, honey?" she asks as she busily does the bookkeeping.

"I'm going to New York."

"Oh, for college? Honey, that's great!" she says, focused.

"No…to find Lily," I say.

"Wha…what? Honey, you make no sense," she replies, finally looking up at me.

"Mom, they aren't finding anything on her or on Frappiero!"

"Honey, they just found out that she is alive on a tape, at a store, and they are trying to track down Frappiero…so give it time!"

"Mom, what kind of security has a girl steal something, have her run out the door, and can't find her? I mean, really! A girl barefoot can't run that far in such short time!" I tell her. A tear streams down her face.

"You're right," she mumbles. "You are right!" she cries. I comfort her for a while.

"Well, I was thinking about flying out to New York City and hunting for clues myself," I say.

"That's so dangerous though. Especially in a big city like that! No, you can't go," she replies.

"But Mom! It's the only way! I can find her...I know I can!"

"No, I lost one daughter. I can't lose another."

"No, Mom, I'm going! I'm eighteen and graduating, so I should have the right to go find my sister!"

"But you will get in the way of the investigation, and then it will take even longer to find her."

"Listen to me!" Tears stream down my face. "I promised myself that I would find her, and I am keeping that promise! I am tired of having this messed-up family mope around and cry when we could put in an effort to find your own fricking daughter! We have all lost it, and you guys don't realize that you would feel so much better if we just had reassurance! We would all feel better if she is home, safe in her bed, covered up in her warm blankets, in her warm house. You haven't been given a fricking wake-up call to see that! Open your darn eyes, Mother! You don't get it that she is right there in front of us; we know where she is, so let's go find her! But no, just go downstairs and clean another flight of stairs or go sign those divorce papers...they are calling your name!" I yell.

"Your father and I are *not* getting a divorce!" she yells back.

"Well, go act like you care about him then! You know he hasn't been home for three days! He is off in Colorado for a business trip, and you probably don't even notice!"

"Don't you dare say that! I love him just as much as anybody else!" she screams. This time she gets up with a wet, streaked face, makeup running down her cheek, and her finger pointing at me.

"Well, Mom! He left to get away from you because he can't stand you anymore. Well, I can't either, so I think it's time I better leave too!" I scream, running down the stairs from the office.

"Macy!" I hear her running down the stairs, so I run to my room. As she gets close, I slam the door in her face. I hear her whimper on the other side, and then I hear her soft footsteps fade away from the door.

I get out my laptop and get on a travel website. I book two plane tickets to New York for the next day at eight in the morning. One ticket is for me and one is for Chelsea. I quickly call her up and tell her that she is flying out with me. She says I'm crazy, but I tell her that she has no choice, and she is the only girlfriend of mine that I can trust. She says her parents (who, by the way, are rich) are off golfing in Florida, so she has to be back in at least a week. She says that she will be in big trouble but that she would take a bullet for me and for my sister. I thank her.

My mom isn't home, but she left a note on the counter. It says that she has left to stay at my grandparents for a while. My mother and her mom (my grandma) are very close. She says that she wants me to be careful and to go find our beautiful angel who has seemed to tear our relationship apart. She wants me to stay strong, and she even drew a heart at the end of the paper.

I begin to pack my bags with casual clothes for some undercover investigating and some dress clothes to go out, since it is the first time that I have ever been to New York! I also pack some pepper spray to keep in my purse in case anyone tries to kidnap me! I also pack my laptops and money that I have saved up from working.

It is kind of weird staying in the house alone. It *is* a big house. I call up Chelsea again, and I go to crash at her place; it will be easier anyway since we are going to the airport in the morning.

⸺◦◉◦⸺

"Yo, yo, yo, baby! I'm *hoooome!*" I yell as I walk into Chelsea's house.

"Upstairs, baby!" she says. I laugh. Calling each other "baby" is our inside joke or nickname for each other. Chelsea is painting her nails in her nice deluxe bathroom.

"Nice color," I remark.

"Why, thank ye," she jokes.

"So are you packed?" I ask.

"Yep, I am packed and ready!" she says. Chelsea is always on top of things, and she is also very organized. Her room and closet are huge since her parents own the country club. Her dad works for Apple Software. I am lucky to have such a good friend.

"So I was wondering...Delaney is having a party at her place; do you want to go?"

"Um...I don't know," I say. I'm not much of a party person. I go out and have fun, sometimes. My parents want me to be social; they don't want me to be a stuck-up party pooper, but they won't let me go to parties with alcohol and, especially, drugs there.

"Do you think there will be any, you know, drinking?" I ask. "Because I'm driving home either way. I'm not drinking, especially with a flight tomorrow." I like to respect my body, and that means no drugs, no smoking, and no driving while intoxicated. My parents taught me well. Chelsea is also a clean person; she respects her body. We are both not boy crazy either. We don't hang with boys that we shouldn't be around, or even girls. We try to stay with a good group like West, Blake, Lena, and of course Chelsea and me.

"Maybe we shouldn't go then," she says. "Hey, wait, there is a party at the country club. It's for Fare (a girl in our grade); they won't allow alcohol or drugs at the country club for underage, and I would know that since my parents own it."

"Okay, that sounds better," I say.

"I bet West will be there, because he is friends with Fare's brother," Chelsea says.

"Yeah, okay! What am I going to wear though? I look too casual with no makeup, T-shirt, shorts, and my hair in a messy bun!" I laugh.

"I'll help you." Chelsea laughs. She leads me to her walk-in closet, which is filled with stylish expensive clothes. She hands me a nice blouse that's a vibrant orange color; it will blend well with my tan. She gives me a soft necklace to go with it. She then hands me some flared Miss Me jeans and a pair of Coach heels that are black snakeskin. She also squirts a little bit of her Jimmy Choo perfume on me. She takes me to her bathroom and does my hair in a nice loose curl and pulls part of my hair back. She gives me a natural look to my makeup, but it shows up nicely. In the end I look like a supermodel. I give her a big hug.

"Thanks for making my day!" I tell her. "After my fight with my mom and everything about my sister, it's been…"

"I know…you don't have to tell me…and don't worry, I understand. Just let it go tonight and don't think about it. We will worry about that stuff tomorrow, but tonight let's just have fun, okay?" she asks.

"Okay," I agree.

We arrive at the country club and walk through security.

"Who has security at a party?" Chelsea laughs.

"Um…rich people with protective parents!" I laugh along with her.

"Well, I guess that makes sense," she says.

I look across the big room with balloons, a full table of desserts and food, streaming lights, and a lot of people.

"Guess a lot of people decided to come here instead of Delaney's, eh?" Chelsea remarks.

"Yeah, and I bet it's safer too!" I reply. Chelsea and I grab some punch, meet the birthday girl, and find a table next to some of our friends.

"Give me all your money!" I hear someone say in my ear. I jump, ready to hit someone. "Wow, it's just me, babe!" West laughs. That's funny because West has never called me "babe" before. I'm quite flattered. I punch his arm jokingly while my friends at the table laugh at my jumpiness.

"You know you can't scare me like that," I say to him over the music.

"Ha-ha-ha…I was just seeing what the gym has been doing to ya," he jokes. "Seeing if you would actually hit someone!" He laughs. I get up from the table and stand by his side. The rest of the table carries on with their own conversations.

"You happy it's Christmas break?" he asks. Suddenly my stomach drops ten floors. I forgot that the other day was our last day of school for Christmas break until January. With me going to New York, I will probably miss Christmas with the rest of my family. I must have been so crazed about this whole sister situation and being in a fight with my mother that I must have forgotten. I wonder what Mom feels like now? Knowing she won't be spending Christmas with either of her daughters. Hopefully Dad will be home in time to be with her…that might be a mess.

"Um…yeah. What about you?" I ask him.

"Yeah. What's on your Christmas list?" he asks.

"Well, for Santa to bring my sister back of course," I reply softly. "What do you want?" I ask.

"You." He winks. I am taken back. Then he nudges me. "I'm just messing with you. I actually want Santa to bring me a new basketball hoop. I kind of wore out the other one." he laughs.

"Oh, that doesn't surprise me!" I laugh.

"Well, listen, I'm actually here with some of my basketball boys so I have to go," he says. "They are waiting on me."

"Oh…okay…well, nice seeing you here," I reply.

"Nice seeing you too!" he says as he walks away. Then he turns around. "Oh…by the way, Macy…you look pretty tonight!"

"Oh, thanks," I say with a big smile. Then he nods and walks out the door.

As I walk to the table, I give Chelsea the scoop on West.

Then she begins to tell me that my ex, Tray, keeps checking me out. Tray was my boyfriend when I was a sophomore. He was my first "serious" boyfriend—if you count only kissing as serious, that is. He is cute but has a big ego. When I found out that he was cheating on me with a girl from another school, I kicked him to the curb.

"Well, I'm *almost* taken…so it sucks to be him," I tell Chelsea, and we start laughing.

"I like how you added the 'almost' in there," she says and laughs.

We end up going home at eleven and set the alarm to wake us up at four o'clock in the morning so we can catch our flight at 8:00 a.m. Not looking forward to that part. Chelsea says that "missing" Christmas with her parents doesn't bother her since they were going to miss Christmas with her anyway just to go golfing. She says that her parents are close to her but are also career oriented, so she doesn't see them a lot. They also like nice things and care more about vacations, but they try their best to take Chelsea with them when they can. Except when they golf. I tell her that I will just send my mom a Christmas present from New York. Maybe time away will be better for my mother and me. As far as my father…I feel sorry for him. This situation has really affected him, so he has been more devoted to his job as a real estate agent.

As I shut off the lights for the night, I get down on my knees and pray. Chelsea is not very open about her religion (at least not to me), but she follows and prays beside me.

"Dear Lord," I begin, "help me keep a level head and do what's right. Keep me strong, and let me bring my sister back into my family's loving arms again. To be able to hold her…

please give me the clues to help me find her and the courage to be brave. Please watch over my family, which is very much falling apart. Help us to take our messed-up puzzle pieces and put them back together—safely, that is—and while you're at it, when you get it together make sure you duct-tape the back so we can never again fall apart." Chelsea lets out a soft laugh.

"I love you. Amen," I say as I get up from my knees.

"You're a strong girl, Macy," Chelsea tells me. "To still have faith after all this…and to still feel the need to get down on your knees and pray. Do you ever feel like giving up?" she asks me.

"Sometimes, but then when I look at one corner with my sister and another corner with the dear Lord, I know that they have my back in this fighting ring. Along with my friends, like you," I say.

"You know it," she says as she hugs me. "I love you…in a 'best friend' way!" she jokes.

"Yeah, me too, and in only a 'best friend' way," I joke along.

My Support System

S tuck in an airport and so tired of everything. I have just enough energy to dress nicely, load my luggage, and get the heck out of this town. Chelsea got stuck in security check because she forgot to take off her charm bracelet even *after* I reminded her! We finally board our flight at 8:45. Chelsea and I sit next to each other while another man in about his late thirties sits on the other side of me.

"Are you going to New York or are you catching another flight?" I ask the man.

"Actually, I live in New York. I'm flying back from visiting my sick mother."

"Oh, I'm sorry," I say. "Well, I'm just going to, um, visit New York."

"Oh...okay...that's cool," he replies.

"Well, not really. I'm actually kind of going there to look for a friend of mine. She went missing a couple months ago, and they sent a whole search party out there for her. Have you heard anything about it?" I ask him.

"Well, I heard a bunch of kids have been kidnapped and

are being blackmailed, but no one can catch them. I actually have a cousin who was kidnapped just two weeks ago. I heard they might be located in New York somewhere," he says.

"Yeah, I have been definitely been doing some of my own undercover investigating," I say.

"Yeah, well, I hope they find your friend," he says.

"Same for your cousin," I say. That is the end of our conversation before he falls asleep to his iPod. I get out my new *Notes and Clues* notebook. I turn to a fresh page and write:

- *More than one kid*
- *Other people have heard about them in New York*

Chelsea is passed out on my shoulder. I really want to text West and tell him that I miss him, but of course we can't have our phones on for a while on the plane.

Finally our flight lands, safely, thank goodness. We go to the luggage pickup and find our bags full of makeup, designer clothes, and hair products. We have to have a *little* fun while we are in the Big Apple, but we have to work hard too. I just wish this was all over. I want her back right now…safe at home. Usually, right now, she would call me telling me to bring her back a souvenir from New York. Only this time I'm praying that *she* is the one I'm bringing back. My parents would usually call me and tell me not to drink and drive and to use my head. Chelsea, meanwhile, is trying to juggle her bags and her phone in one hand; she is talking to her mom.

"Yeah, OK…OK, Mom! I promise I'll be careful. Yes, I'm sorry. Love you to. Bye," she says.

"She's mad that I am missing Christmas, even though I'll

be spending it alone, and she's still mad at me for telling her last night that I was leaving for New York."

"Ha-ha, well, I can try to save your butt. When we rescue my sister, your mommy will think that you're a hero!" I joke.

"Ha-ha, got that right!" she says.

We get a cab and are driven to the city. We book a room in a Marriott hotel. It's super expensive, but I decide to use my credit card from my parents and pay it off later. I unpack my clothes and my laptops. Chelsea lies on her own queen-size bed.

"This is kind of relaxing," she says.

"Seriously, Chelsea. We aren't here to relax" I say.

"Well...I know, but I have never been to New York before either," she says.

"Yeah, well, get some nice clothes on; we are going out to eat for supper."

"Wow, it's already five?" she asks.

"Yeah," I say.

She gets out of bed and plugs in her curling iron. I turn on my laptops. One I have on my Facebook page, the other on a list of missing children in the United States.

"Okay, Chelsea, the man sitting next to us on the plane said he has a cousin missing as well. I think he or she was kidnapped by the same person as my sister," I tell her.

"Well, you don't know that for sure though," she says.

"We'll see; it's a guess or a 'gut' feeling. So I am thinking there are more kids kidnapped by him than just my sister."

"Okay, that seems reasonable," Chelsea says.

"Yes, so I am going to uncover these missing children's identities and where they might be now," I tell her.

"Um…how are you going to do that exactly?" she asks me.

"Well, I already have details about what they look like and where they were last seen from this web page. So now comes the fun part," I tell her.

"Oooh, SHOPPING!" she screams.

I punch her in the arm. "No, stupid, undercover investigating!" I say. "Oh, and you need to be quiet; we do have people sleeping next door."

"And how would you know if they are sleeping or not? Do you secretly do undercover investigating on them too?" she jokes.

"Perhaps!" I laugh even though it isn't true. "Okay, so here is what we are going to do. I am going to call each of these numbers on the 'Have You Seen This Child?' sheet. It says here that if you call in to this missing child hotline number, they can give you an update on the whereabouts of the missing child. So if I call in asking about all of these children and the latest evidence found on them, I could get further along in this case. Do you understand me?" I ask her.

"Yeah, how do you think up all of this?" she asks me.

"When it's all you think about, you have to come up with some ideas sometime," I say. "All right…now I don't think any of the search party or the undercover cops down here know that I am here. I know they won't mind me helping them find my own sister, but what I will be doing might go too far into their own work."

"Okay, so what are you saying?" Chelsea asks.

"I am saying that I will have to dress up as a different person so the search party or the cops do not know who I am, even though they have never met me except for the two officers back home. I don't want them mistaking me for my sister because we do look alike."

"Oh, now you make sense," she tells me.

Later that day we go shopping at a wig store, a make-up store, a lot of clothing and shoes stores, along with a Christmas store to buy my parents a Christmas gift. I make sure I wear a hat so no one can see my hair or face. We go back to our hotel room and organize all of our new merchandise. Thank the Lord that I still have enough money left. I did use a coupon book, and I only used cash so my credit card would be safe. I got some good deals too. Chelsea is passed out on her bed.

"Chelsea, get up!" I joke.

"Screw you!" she yells through her pillow.

"Hey, come on. We're in the city that never sleeps," I say as I start jumping on her bed.

"If we get kicked out of this place from you being loud, I am *not* sleeping on a bench out in the street," she yells.

"Ha-ha, don't worry, we will just take the sheets and blankets with us, and it will be all good," I joke.

"Um…yeah, until I have a stranger snuggling up next to me," she says and laughs.

"Well, while you are sleeping, I will be on the phone to the hotline doing my undercover investigation," I tell her.

"Okay, have fun," she says, and then she is out, snoring away.

I reopen my laptop and dial the hotline number. I decide to check on a girl named Sabrina Hope. She is twelve on this missing sheet, and she was at a public park on the Fourth of

July when she was taken hostage. Her mother did not have a close enough eye on her.

Hotline:	"Missing Child Crisis Hotline, this is Christina. How may I help you?"
Me:	"I am Jane Faith and I was wondering about the investigation of Sabrina Hope?"
Hotline:	"Well, what exactly do you want to know, miss?"
Me:	"Are there any certain pieces of evidence they have found or have they located her yet?"
Hotline:	"Yes, they have found some surveillance videos of her stealing video games and food out of stores. We tracked the latest video to New York City. The police could not find a trace of her after the alarms were triggered, but some witnesses saw her getting in an old red van. The witnesses say they think it was a Dodge driven by a man in his early twenties, but the van sped off so fast that the witnesses didn't see where it went after it made a left turn from the parking lot.
Me:	"Okay, did she have a Facebook page?"
Hotline:	"Yes."
Me:	"All right. Well, thank you. I saw her on the missing list, and I was curious about her case. I will keep my eye out. Thank you."
Hotline:	"No problem, have a nice day."

I hang up the phone. The lady probably thought it was weird that I just called in because I'm curious about Sabrina's case, but, oh well... I am figuring this out to help the missing cases. I may end up rescuing her as well. On my notes I add:

- *Sabrina Hope is also "maybe" another victim of the same kidnapper. They also think she is located in New York. Also stealing things from stores in New York like my sister. Again police could not catch them. Old, red Dodge van. Driver early twenties.*

"I like your fake name," Chelsea says to me.

"Oh, you're awake," I say.

"Yeah, I heard you over the phone...sounds like we have more clues," she says.

"Yeah, but still not enough," I reply. "Well, at least we know she is with a group. The more people she is with, probably the less they will pay attention to her, as for abuse."

"We only hope that they don't abuse her! If they are, they are so going to pay!" she says.

"Oh, more than that. I'll punch them so hard it will knock them into tomorrow!" I say as I crack my knuckles viciously.

"Okay, calm down. Let's not get to violent here," Chelsea says.

"Sorry, it's just all the anger built up inside of me," I tell her. Oh no, here come the tears. "I just hate to see my family like this; it just hurts me so much. I am so worried about her, Chelsea. I can't sleep, eat, or even think about anything else but her," I complain to Chelsea. She pulls me in tight and lets me cry on her shoulder.

"I know…I know. You know, you are handling this much better than I would have if my oldest brother went missing," she says.

"What! Look at me though; I am a train wreck! I look like crap, and I feel like crap," I tell her.

"No you don't. In my eyes I don't care what you look like, and when you don't feel good, I understand. We all have bad times, Macy, but we need good friends and a good support system to help us get over those times. So I am always here for you, no matter what," she tells me.

"Thanks, Chelsea, that means a lot," I say as I blow my nose.

"Ha ha, no problem. Now go take a shower and go to sleep; you need it!" she tells me.

"Okay, will do." I laugh. From that moment on, I know who my true friend is. She's always there when others aren't, helps me make the right decisions, and keeps me grounded. She always throws that smile back onto my face. Chelsea is my support system.

You Could Be Anywhere by Now

I wake up to sunshine peeking through our hotel curtains. It is already nine o'clock. I wake up Chelsea.

"It's time," I tell her. She jumps out of bed and calls up for breakfast. Then she runs to the bathroom.

"This is so exciting," she tells me.

"Yeah, sure, but don't make me look funny or scary!" I say. She shakes her head and picks out a nice blouse that I bought, skinny jeans, and some Mary Jane's (that she bought herself) and makes me put them on. Then she throws my hair back, pins it up, and wraps this thin, sticky stuff around it. She picks up my blonde, loosely curled wig and throws it on my head. She places it neatly. Then she does my makeup, adding some brown eye shadow and a light pink to the eyelids. She adds brown mascara and pink lipstick. Oh, and before she did my makeup, she had me put some blue-colored contacts in since my actual eye color is hazel.

"There you go, ma'am." She shows me off in the full mirror. "A new girl you are!" she says. "Now think of your new name."

"Um…how about Annabelle Rain?" I ask.

"Good! It's unique; I haven't heard of the last name 'Rain' before," she says.

"Okay, well, I guess that's my new name. Now I don't look anything like my sister; hopefully no one will ask me about her," I say.

"I hope not either…she has been on the news a lot," Chelsea says.

"I know, and it's driving me crazy having people want to interview me about how I feel when I feel utterly confused at this state. I mean, why of all things would this happen to me?"

"I don't know, maybe God's trying to make you stronger," she replies.

"You know what? I am thinking the same thing," I tell her.

We eat our breakfast and then head down to the lobby to catch a cab. I plan on going to the place where my sister robbed the video game and tracking down the roads from there. It is gently snowing outside, and the aisles of skyscrapers are all neatly decorated with the Christmas spirit. The cab takes us to the Walmart in Secaucus, about eight miles from New York. Chelsea and I, not wanting to look suspicious, bought a pack of gum at Walmart and headed off on our search. The Walmart store is located on Park Plaza Drive, which could lead into the New Jersey Turnpike (Interstate 95). So he could have had Sabrina rob a store in New York City, take off to Secaucus, and rob Walmart on the way. Then he could have taken off onto Interstate 95 where the cops would have to chase him down at top speed.

"So they very well could be out of New Jersey by now," I tell Chelsea.

"Um…you think?" she replies sarcastically. I put my head in my hands and sigh.

"I am so confused!" I say. "How are we ever going to track them down when they hightailed it on the interstate to who knows where!"

"Yeah, it's hard because they could have gone anywhere on the interstate." she says.

"Ugh, I know! I thought we really had a big clue coming with the street locations, but I guess not," I say. Chelsea and I end up calling the cab that brought us to pick us back up. He drives us back to our hotel, and I pay him, giving him a generous tip. The snow is now blanketing the sidewalks, and my winter coat is now white. The city is so pretty, but I feel so small. It is a beautiful view though, snow sprinkling down on this big city with its big skyscrapers. Chelsea snaps a photo of us together, pink faced from the coldness. That's not the only thing that feels cold; my heart does as well. My love for people has turned to hatred, and my compassion has turned to sorrow. I can't trust anyone but Chelsea. I don't understand the world anymore. What is wrong with people nowadays? Can't they just live life and enjoy themselves? But no. They are money-hungry animals who can't get their minds straight. Someone took away my sister's freedom just for money or for nice things that they can't buy or afford. Someone took my sister's precious time to instead blackmail her and make her a slave. How dare they ever look in the mirror at themselves and feel that they are OK! They are truly wrong and have sinned. We all make mistakes, but it is up to us to learn from them.

Chelsea and I head into Starbucks and get a salted caramel hot chocolate. We sit and chat for a while about how our parents have been and what we want to do in life. I tell her at this point I don't really know. I wanted to go to school for fine arts, but after this rampage, I feel the need to slack. My grades have been staying pretty average now, since I have learned that even though my sister is gone, I still need my education. I know my sister would still want me to succeed in what I do best. So I keep studying and trying my best. I'm still thinking about doing track in the spring. I also did cheerleading for a while and was quite entertained by it, especially with my gymnastics background, but I had to quit when Lily went missing. Along with volleyball and gymnastics, the only sport I have taken up again since her disappearance.

A few hours after Starbucks and after touring the city, Chelsea reports to me that she is hungry.

"You're actually hungry?" I ask her.

"Um…yeah. It's five o'clock! Let's go to one of those piano jazz bars," she says.

"Why there?" I ask.

"Because I have never been to one," she says.

"Well, we can't get an alcoholic drink so we will have to settle for something else to drink," I say.

"Okay…if you say so," she says.

"Oh, and you're paying," I add.

"Deal!" she says, and we hop in another taxicab.

The bar is nice and clean and has a mini stage with a grand piano on it. Some dude is playing a soft melody that would put a person to sleep. Chelsea and I both order Shirley Temples and a chicken salad.

"Hey, you should go up and sing," she tells me. I have always loved to sing, and I often would sing at talent shows for our school.

"I don't know, Chelsea..." I begin.

"Oh, come on. You have a great voice, and besides, that man is putting these people to sleep!" she tells me.

"Oh, okay," I say. Chelsea runs up to a man peeking out from behind the backstage curtain. She whispers something to him and he nods.

"Okay, let's go!" she says as she pulls my arm. The man says I can play one song since the man at the piano is just a volunteer.

I go up to the microphone and introduce myself as Annabelle, and then I begin playing "Love Song" from Sarah Bareilles on the piano. I start singing as I gently glide my fingers on the keys:

"I'm not gonna write you a love song 'cause ya asked for it, 'cause ya need one, you see..."

Soon I am done...not even missing a note vocally nor on the piano. I am pretty proud of myself. I am presented with a huge applause from the audience, especially from Chelsea.

Later that night, back at the hotel:

"Why don't you sing much anymore?" Chelsea asks me.

"Oh, I don't know," I say. "I sing to myself, but you know, ever since she has been gone I haven't gotten out in public a lot. All I see is people talking about my sister and how hard it is on my family and me. Also the rumors people spread about my family and me only add up to more drama in our situation."

"Yeah, I understand," she tells me. As she turns off the

light, I look out at the city. It's so big that Lily could get lost even a block away from where we are. That scares me; it feels like a stab in the heart—a feeling that once again makes me carry a burden of sadness on my shoulders. And it just keeps pushing down.

I Now Know

It's Christmas Eve today, and I miss you. I'm here in New York looking for you. I will find you and bring you home, I promise. Try anything to get away from the people who have you held hostage. Get to a nearby telephone and call me as soon as you can, and then stay with the police until I come and get you. I love you sooo much.

Love,
Macy

I tie the letter to a balloon and set it free into the wind. I watch it fly over the skyscrapers in the center of the city. A tear slides down my face, but I gently wipe it away. I am hoping she may receive this even though it is very doubtful. It just gives me a better feeling in my mind and in my heart.

Chelsea and I went shopping today for a gift for my parents. I decided to give them something that would give them some hope about my sister. I bought a picture frame for them that is silver with one pink diamond, shaped into a heart that is built into the frame. It has the saying "Gone but not forgotten" on it. The pink heart is replacing the "o" in "Gone."

I decide to go to a printing shop (since I brought my camera and card) and print off the picture of my sister and me on the Fourth of July. It is an outstanding picture that my mom took of us right when the fireworks blasted in the night sky. Lily looks so happy and delicate in that picture. She was always so delicate in my eyes. I was so gentle with her and was always overly protective. It only took that one day for me to lose her.

Chelsea thinks it is a nice idea and that it will mean a lot to my parents. I wrap it up and put it in a shipping box along with a Christmas card.

Dear Mom and Dad,

I will be home shortly. I will bring you back news, but for now it is too long to tell you in letter or on the phone. It is very hard to explain. You will need a map to understand me when I tell you about my discovery. Sorry I could not be there for Christmas; tell everyone hello. It is for the best. Take care.

Love,
Macy

I ask the shipping company for immediate shipping. It costs a lot more, but, oh well, it's worth it.

Chelsea bought her parents golfing hats.

Chelsea and I for Christmas Eve celebrate by going to a Christmas caroling production and then going out to a

cheesecake restaurant where we have hot cocoa and pepper-
mint cheesecake. We are both asleep by ten o'clock. We are
sure party animals, aren't we?

I awake to all the church bells ringing in the city.
It sounds beautiful. Chelsea is up as well, and we get
dressed. I give her the present I bought her yesterday
while shopping; it's a pink snakeskin purse with the letter
"C" embroidered on it. She loves it. She gives me another
charm to go on my charm bracelet. The charm is a pink
heart diamond and it says BFFs on it. I truly love it. As
we are getting ready to go down to the lobby, I receive a
phone call. It's from West.

"Hello?" I answer.

"Hey, it's me…how are you?" he asks.

"Oh, hey, I'm doing all right. Chelsea is keeping me in a
good mood," I joke.

"Ha-ha…I'm sure! How's NYC?"

"Oh, it's good. Definitely a busy environment. It's hard to
get around here," I say.

"I'm sure…well, Merry Christmas!" he says.

"Ha-ha, thanks…you too," I reply.

"When will you be back?" he asks.

"Um…we are flying out sometime tomorrow," I say.

"Oh, gotcha. Well, I got to go, but I figured I would call
you so…see ya!" he says.

"Bye," I say as we hang up. I also talk to my mom on
the phone. She says that she misses me and that my dad got
home safely from his trip. I can still hear the sadness in her
voice, but I'm not going to bring that part up. I tell her a bit
about my discovery at Walmart but not all of it. I don't need

her worrying on Christmas. I tell her that I love her and that I will be home soon.

Chelsea and I decide to go walk the streets a bit and see all of the decorations again. We can't spend a lot of money on shows, since we have spent most of it on our hotel, food, taxis, and shopping.

We decide to go walk past a strip mall when in the alley I see a little girl about twelve hunched over and crying. I whisper to Chelsea. We decide to help her out. As I walk up to her, she looks familiar. My jaw instantly drops. It's Sabrina Hope! I drop down beside her, trying to keep calm. My heart is racing.

"Excuse me, who are you?" I ask. I probably sound stupid.

"I…I'm Sabrina Ho…Hope," she says between the chattering of her teeth from the cold. Chelsea gets wide eyed.

"I know who you are, and I can help you," I tell her.

"How do you kn…know me?" she asks.

"I saw you on the missing children list," I say.

"Oh… please help…help me," she cries.

"First of all, we have to take you to the police," I tell her. "They will take you back home."

She starts to cry. "Oh please! Please take me home!" she cries. I can't ask her any questions right now…the poor girl is freezing! I know I have to turn her in and get her calm before I can ask her what has happened.

Chelsea is on the phone with 911 and reports that she has found a missing child. We are told to stay where we are. It's not even ten minutes before the police and ambulances arrive. They load the girl in one car and Chelsea and me in another.

We have to answer where we found her and how. Chelsea and I also have to answer other brief questions. I have to explain to them about my missing sister and why I am in New York. While I am explaining, the cops are looking up my sister's case. I hear crying in the other room. Sabrina's parents are rejoined with her for the first time in a long time. They are hugging her so tight. They are so happy that I also began to cry. The parents thank me over and over again. They say that I am their hero and that I am an angel. After the police interviewed Sabrina and her family, I am allowed to ask Sabrina questions myself.

I start by telling Sabrina how my sister went missing and how I was able to track this Frappiero guy over Facebook. I explain how I came to New York to find my sister and to get clues about her case. I ask her if she was with my sister?

She tells me that she was kidnapped by Frappiero and another guy named Brian. They saw her getting out of school when they asked her to come with them, and they showed her a gun in their pocket. They told her that if she said one word, they would harm her family. She thought she could run away when they weren't looking or jump out of the car, but she thought wrong. When they threw her in their beat-up red van, she was thrown in with other kids her age. There were three girls and four boys; she made the fourth girl. She and the rest of the kids were tied up with ropes and had their mouths duct-taped shut. She tells me that this happened to her before my sister was kidnapped. Sabrina is from Colorado, and in order for Frappiero and Brian not to get caught, they had to drive to Oklahoma. The kids were hunched and tied down to the seats so no one from the outside could see them. She remembers how painful the ride was with the kids crying and being stuck in an uncomfortable position. After they made it to Oklahoma, they stayed in an old abandoned building in Oklahoma City. They carried all the kids inside. The place was dirty, and there was rat poop everywhere. All of the windows were broken and the floor was dusty. She thinks it used to be an old glove factory. Brian untied the other kids and gave them all one slice of pizza from Casey's that they had ordered, while Frappiero took Sabrina into another room. She was afraid that he was going to harm her in different ways, but instead he just sat her down in a chair and sat the gun on a small table in front of him. Apparently he had been in the abandoned building before. He told her that he had kidnapped her because he needed her help on stealing. He told her that he couldn't afford money for video games or stuff that he wants; he could only afford so much food. He explained to her that she must do what he asks, or he will drop her off on the street in the middle of nowhere to starve. He told her that he does not beat anybody unless they do not do something he has asked of them. He said that he would feed her only to stay conscious so she would be able to go on the run and steal things. He told her that she had to steal the things he wanted, otherwise he would hurt her and her family. There would be no chickening out.

That night she slept on the cold floor with all of the other children while Brian and Frappiero set out their game plan for the next day. Their plan was to have Sabrina go into the game store a couple blocks away, steal the video game they wanted, and have her jump back in the vehicle out front.

They would speed out of the parking lot and take an interstate or highway that would lead them to Iowa. That's how it happened the next day; their plan had worked.

She says that they kidnapped my sister the same way. Except when they kidnapped my sister, Frappiero went to buy movie tickets at the local movie theater where I worked. He bought the movie tickets to make it look like a cover-up if the cops asked him where he was on October 17.

When Sabrina tells me this, it all clicks in my head. When Frappiero got out of his car at the movie theater, Lily's shoe must have fallen out of her gym bag. Maybe Lily's gym bag was up in the front seat with Frappiero (maybe he thought he could steal something), but one of the shoes fell out when Frappiero got out of the car. Later on I had been the one to find it.

One thing I kept thinking about was if I remembered waiting on Frappiero at the movie theater. Of course I was working that day, but I apparently didn't notice him. Thinking of that creeps me out.

Sabrina goes on to tell me that my sister had to sit by her for the entire ride to Illinois after leaving the movie theater. The kids were only allowed to talk to each other when they ate, that is, if Brian was watching them. They only received one meal a day and it was fast food in small portions. Sabrina only asked Lily her name, and that was all they ever said. Lily had to talk to Frappiero, just like Sabrina had to, but this time in an old abandoned building in Chicago. Sabrina tells me that Lily tried to stay calm, but you could tell through everyone's duct-taped mouths at night that Lily was scared. You could hear her sigh heavy, deep breaths that were full of sadness and heartbreak, she tells me. They had another kid rob a store in Chicago, and then they moved on to other states, having the kids rob either a video game store or an electronic store without getting caught. Sabrina still wonders how they could never get caught, but they always chose a store next to an interstate so they could get away fast enough.

Sabrina tells me how a month later Lily still hadn't had to rob any stores, and they were both dramatically skinny from not eating enough. Finally they ended up in New York where they stayed in yet another abandoned building in the rundown side of New York. Sabrina was told that day to rob a store close to downtown. She came running out of the store, and instead of running to the car, she ran in the opposite direction. Frappiero chased her down in the car, jumped out, and grabbed her by the arm. He pushed her hard to the ground, picked her up by her feet, and threw her into an alleyway where he left her. Frappiero, Brian, and the other kids took off. After they had abandoned her, she was too scared to ask for help or to trust anybody. She was afraid that who ever tried to help her would use her like Frappiero and Brian did. Instead she ate leftover garbage out of dumpsters and slept in alleyways at night to hide from investigators looking for her. She says that before I found her, she was tired of hiding and was so hungry that she just stayed out in the middle of the alleyway. She hoped someone would see her. She thanks me for noticing her and helping her.

As Sabrina is telling me her story, I am crying on Chelsea's shoulder. I can't help to think about how my sister is with those crazy, sick people living in abandoned buildings in a dangerous city. I miss her so much that my stomach is turning sour, and the story I am hearing is driving me insane! At the same time, I am happy someone told me. I finally have a witness to tell me what happened. I needed someone to tell me that my sister is not being beaten or abused. It hurts me to know that she is hardly fed, sleeping on floors with duct-tape over her mouth, and being with total strangers that force her to do things that she is not willing to do.

After we all sit there in silence for a while, except for me crying in the corner, I have enough guts to ask her.

"Sabrina..." I begin, "tell me she's alive."

Sabrina grabs my arm and holds it. "She is alive, I'm sure of it, but I haven't seen her for a week. I'm positive that she is still alive."

My breath is taken away, and I fall out of my chair. Chelsea leans down to help me up, but I am too limp. I just bow down on my knees and cry. I am crying harder than I have in a long time. The tears streak my face; I am so happy to know that she is out there somewhere. I grab Sabrina with all of the strength I have left, and I hug her. I am crying too hard to give her a thank-you. She gently cries with me, though her tears are not as dramatic as mine. Chelsea is next to me telling me to breathe.

"She...she...she's...alive, Chel...sea!" I cry to her.

"I know," she says as she cries along with me. Soon everybody is crying. There are both happy and sad tears. I know that I have a chance to find her and bring her back home. That she is alive and still breathing that precious oxygen. Though the thought of her being skinny, dirty, and living in the condition that she is in right now hurts me. It hurts me so bad, that it is like a stab in the heart. It's not that I couldn't keep her safe enough! Why did God think that my parents or I couldn't take care of her? We fed her, bathed her, kept her company, and treated her with respect. She had no right to lose that privilege! Those people had no right to take her from me like this. They are selfish, selfish people! If they could see me right now, I'd show them exactly how I feel. When so much is being pushed upon your shoulders, there is a time when you collapse from the weight. The weight doesn't have to be caused by more than one thing; one person can even cause it, and that is what makes life not fair. I know God made this happen for a reason…to make my family stronger. To also make me stronger and to be able to fight off the easy things in life, like not getting concert tickets to Katy Perry for my sixteenth birthday or not getting the job at a clothing store. This, though, is far from that. Those are the days when just missing a concert was bad news to me. I made such a big fit about it, and now when I look back, I look stupid because here I am today crying over my sister who I haven't seen in almost three months…that's unfair!

After Chelsea helps me wipe my tears, I have to talk with some police about being on a court trial as a witness. After that I have to break the news to my parents. My mom is relieved that they think she is still alive, and we know how she was kidnapped. My dad is very upset like me; how could someone be sick enough to take her hostage.

After I set up a court date, Chelsea and I decide that we have had enough drama for one day. We go back to our hotel and pack up, ready to catch our flight for tomorrow. It hasn't been the best Christmas ever, but at least a family is getting to spend it with their daughter whom they haven't seen in a long time. I am glad I found Sabrina; I have learned a lot more.

In the morning our flight takes off at nine o'clock. We are up and around about five and get there to check in with security. Our flight is kind of relaxing, after all of the stress we have had, but the airport is packed since everyone is flying out or flying back from Christmas. I write down everything that Sabrina told me the other day in my notebook, just to keep track of the details.

I can't believe I am saying this, but I am kind of ready to be home again. Usually I don't want to be home. I don't want to deal with my family's problems, but I actually kind of miss them. I am ready to be home in my own bed, and I think Chelsea feels the same way. No matter who you are or where you come from, you always still love your family. Even if there are days when you feel like you don't, remember that they brought you into this world…so you are kind of stuck with them. ☺

I Am Ready

Home, I am home. I'm asleep in my own bed, with the comfort of my own sheets and the smell of my mom's burning candle.

I had a dream—not a Martin Luther King dream, no. I had a dream that I was face-to-face with this man; he wanted money. I was to give him money only for something in exchange, but I did not know what it was.

I'm awakened after I hear my mother and father in the living room talking. I get up, put my hair in a ponytail, and go out to greet them. They are sitting by the Christmas tree drinking coffee together. Just seeing them in the same room surprises me, let alone having coffee together!

"Hello, dear," my mother says to me.

"Um…hi," I say, still a little bit uncomfortable around her since our fight.

"We decided that today we would have you open your gifts from Christmas, even though Christmas was yesterday," my dad says.

"Um…sure," I reply.

SISTER STRONG

An hour later I have all of my gifts in a pile. I got some more makeup, clothes, and another charm for my bracelet, which is an angel. On the angel it says in tiny letters, "God bless my sister." That's my favorite gift of all. I thank them, and then I have a cup of hot chocolate. It seems to soothe my stress.

Later that day I take many naps and eat a lot. I am still fighting a bit of jet lag from the trip, and I just want to enjoy my day at home. It is a relaxing day.

It's Sunday and I attend church for the first time in a while. It is actually great to be back. I thought at first that people would stare at us and wonder in curiosity about our problems, but they didn't. A lot of people actually come up to us and tell us that they are praying for us. They say that they support us and to call them if we need anything. It makes me feel good inside, that people are there for us. Also that even when you have down times and you think people don't care about you, they do. For instance, let's say you don't have a lot of friends you talk to at school, but when your house burns down, soon all of your friends are there to have your back. They help you and your family get back on their feet. That's what true friends are.

Going to church makes me realize that they want to help us and to make us feel happy again. I know that I have a lot of people supporting us, and it's a good feeling.

After I come home, I decide that I will be strong through all of this. I will try anything to get her back if it is the last thing I do. I pray to the Lord to give me courage, to guide me in the right direction, because what I am going to do is probably the most insane thing I have ever done in my whole life. Imagine this, it all came in a dream.

I log on to my Facebook page at 3:00 a.m., knowing that he is setting up his plan. Frappiero knows that people are searching for him, so he deactivates his Facebook account. I decide to look up Brian's profile. Instead of friending him right away, I send him a message:

Me: …I know you have my sister, Lily. You kidnapped her almost four months ago. I want her back! I am willing to give you one million dollars in exchange for Lily. I promise you that I will have the money on time, and you promise me you won't hurt my sister. —Macy

Brian replies an hour later.

Brian: I have your sister alive right now. No need to worry, but I want the money and the correct amount of money! I will give your sister, Lily, in exchange for two million dollars. Deal?

Me: Deal! But you have to promise me that she will not be harmed in any way until I have her in my hands. And I promise that I will keep the cops off your back, and I will give you the correct amount of money. It will not be stolen money either. Deal?

Brian: Deal! I will give you a month to get the money, so that gives me a month to get back to the location where we will meet. Where is our meeting spot?

Me: We will meet at the abandoned building where you stayed in New York. That's right, I know where you have been! So give me directions, and we meet there on February first. If you are a no-show, I will have the cops hunt you down. We will meet face-to-face, which means you and only you will be handing over my sister, and I will be handing over the money "to you" and only you. There will be no weapons allowed, meaning no handguns, knives, chain saws, pencils, or anything that may harm someone. Just bring yourself and my sister to the location. Do I make myself clear?

Brian: Yes, you are heard clear. I will bring only your sister and myself to the location. And you better be there with the money or I will hurt you and your family, and I will hurt your precious little sister too! As long as I have the money, I will give you back your sister. We will be meeting on February first at 5:00 p.m. at the abandoned building a block down from the Walmart in Secaucus, New York. On the front of the building, it will have a slab of concrete with a date on it. That is how you will know it is the right one. We will meet inside.

Me: It is a deal! No backing out either!

Brian: Deal...no backing out. See you then, with my money!

My heart is racing. The only reason why Brian still has Facebook is because he doesn't think the police are onto him yet, just Frappiero. I am now going to get her back, finally! I still have one thing to do. I run up to my mom's office and print off our e-mail conversation. I paper-clip the papers together and run downstairs to find my parents. My mom is washing the dishes, and my dad is reading the paper. I tell them that we need to go to the station right away. They want an explanation, but I tell them I am not giving them one until they come with me. I also tell them that this is very important; it is about Lily. As soon as I say that, they hop in the car and take me to the station.

We sit down again with Officer Cane and Officer Wellis. I dig out the printed papers of the e-mail conversation that I had with Brian. I tell them to get out their files about the story Sabrina told us after I found her. I explain to them about my dream and about how I was in contact once with Frappiero on Facebook, which they already know. I tell them how Frappiero deactivated his account but Brian is still on Facebook. I also tell them my latest mission to New York. They read through the e-mail messages and tell me that I am doing everything wrong. They say that it is too dangerous to step into this situation. They say that they would have to track them down at least a month before I went. Then I tell them my plan.

I tell them that my plan, on February first, is to meet Brian in the listed location on the e-mail and give him the money. In return I will get my sister back. Meanwhile I will have the police and a SWAT team in hiding, not in the building or outside the building, but around a block or so. When I hand him over the money and after he hands over my sister, I will send them a sign. The sign will alert the SWAT team, meaning that I am ready for them to take over the building, take Brian hostage, and arrest him. I will have the police take my sister and me out safely. Therefore, he will be arrested and will get no part in the money that I had promised him.

They all look at me in awe. "How did you think of all of this?" they ask me.

"I don't know. It just comes naturally to me. I am constantly thinking of ways to solve problems, and ever since she went missing, I have been thinking of ways to rescue her," I tell them.

They explain to me that they will have to talk it over with their boss and the government to make sure that it is the right thing to do. They will keep us in contact, and to be able to catch them this way, we will have to have many more meetings.

My parents are so impressed by my idea that they take me out to dinner, so they can get more details on it. We have to brainstorm ideas on how to get two million dollars in a month, which will be super hard. Unless, somehow, the government allows us to borrow two million to give to Brian as a cover-up and then give the money back to the government after we arrest Brian. I'm not sure if that's even possible. What if Brian gets away? Besides, I would rather just earn my own money so I can keep it in the end. My parents suggest having a fund-raiser at my church, getting another job, or becoming famous. The whole famous part, well, they are joking. But it gives me an idea of getting back into music and starting to write songs. They say that if that happens, I can maybe have a concert at my school and raise money. As we are talking, my dad informs me that if the authorities confirm my plan, I will need to get stronger. He means both physically and emotionally. He reminds me that even though Brian promises he will just bring himself and my sister, we can trust no one. We are betting that he will bring Frappiero along as well. My dad also tells me that once Brian gets the money, he will be on the run. He says that he wants to start training me; he want's me to hit the gym again. He says that in a month he should have me ripped. I already have muscle, so as soon as I double my workouts, it will take me no time to get bulky.

I am ready for this step. I am ready to take these challenges: having meetings, working out all the time, and being able to come face-to-face with my sister's kidnapper. I will do whatever it takes, no matter how much pain is involved, to get my sister back. My dad tells me that I will need to start target practicing and shooting his handgun. Even though I am not allowed weapons at the location, he still wants me to take one. He thinks that if Brian had enough guts to kidnap my sister, he has enough guts to break our rules and shoot me. I can't let my parents live with that drama. I agree with my dad, and I tell him that I would love it if he would train me. I think this is what I need.

My mom tells me that she will help me with the fundraising part; she has good ideas. I am anxious about this. I just want Lily back now! I tell myself that I need to be strong and patient though, that the day will come.

I go to bed with my head spinning. I have so much to

think about. I can't sleep a wink. I am scared, but I'm ready. I am ready to finally see her again, to hug her and kiss her again, and to be able to talk, laugh, and joke with her again. I want to cry with her again. I am ready.

Not Giving Up

My dad wakes me up. "Get up! Let's go! Let's go!" he yells in my ear.

"What are you doing?" I moan, still half asleep.

"You are hitting the gym...*now!*" he yells.

"Ugh, seriously, Dad! It's 6:30 in the morning," I cry.

"I don't care whether it's 6:30 in the morning or 6:30 at night, let's go! Get some workout clothes on and meet me downstairs in the fitness room," he yells.

I am seriously second-guessing myself at this point. Do I really want to do this? But then I remember my sister; I remember that I need to fight for her sake. I can fight through this.

My dad was in the military before my sister was born. Now he is a real estate agent, but he is still pretty strict, and for a forty-plus-year-old man, he has nice muscles. He still works out when he has time. I used to work out with him until high school when I started lifting at the school's gym. The fitness room in our house is the size of two of my bedrooms put together. It has everything from a TV, a treadmill, lifting sets, and dumbbells, to a roomy area for workout videos.

I like using the school's fitness room better since I can work out with my friends.

After changing into my workout clothes, I walk downstairs to our fitness room. My dad is there waiting for me.

"Today, you will hate me, but I just want you to remember that this will only make you stronger. Now I want you to stretch out, meaning do all of your gymnastics stretches or anything that will get your body stretched out so you don't pull anything…got me?" he asks.

"Yeah," I reply as I start stretching. Maybe this won't be too bad.

Fifteen minutes later, I shouldn't have jinxed it.

"All right, I want you to run two miles," he tells me. "The first mile will be a steady pace to warm up; the second mile will be partially sprinting (on a fast-paced run). If you stop, walk, or jog on the second mile, you owe me fifty push-ups."

"Are you kidding me?" I remark.

"No, I am not kidding you, so get your butt on that treadmill and start running!" he yells to me. "Your steady pace will be 5-5.5 mph and your sprint will be 6.5-7 mph, OK?" he asks me.

"Yeah, I understand," I say.

I track two miles into the system and set the alarm to beep at a mile— that way I know when I should change my pace. I start off. It's not too hard until I reach four minutes; I'm a few minutes off from my first mile. Keeping my breathing steady is hard, especially from all the weight I gained in New York; it wasn't a lot, but I still feel heavy. I don't recommend trying any of these workouts without a personal trainer assisting you.

My dad watches me like a hawk. As soon as I am on my second mile, I feel like I am going to puke. Every time I try to put my hands on the handlebars my dad slaps them, hard! He tells me to be a fighter, not a sissy. My heart is on fire, and my throat is dry. My legs feel tight and sore. I haven't run this hard since track season, which will be here soon in March. My body is on fire, and when the treadmill finally beeps, telling me I have finally completed my mile, I clasp right onto the treadmill. No, I do not faint. I'm just too tired to stand up, so I sit down on the edge of the treadmill trying to catch my breath. Being on a dead run for a whole mile is very difficult. I usually run the fifteen hundred in track, and that isn't even as hard as sprinting a whole mile.

"Get up…there is no sitting in this workout…*ever!*" my dad yells at me. I slowly get up and reach for the water he is holding. He again slaps my hand. His slaps don't hurt, and he doesn't mean them to hurt, but it is enough for me to know that he means business.

"You will learn self discipline. When your brain is needy for something, you need to learn to control your first aggression. You will need to show me that you can work hard enough, and when I see that, I will reward you with water. Now, to show me how much you want this water, you have to do fifty push-ups. They need to be in good form: no stopping, your chest must touch, and if it does not, then you will do them all over again, no matter how tired you are," he tells me. He gives me a head nod, and I know it is time to start.

I get down in push-up position and start pumping them out. All of them seem to be in good form. My arms start getting tired at thirty and they began to shake. My dad is yelling at me to keep my butt tight and my elbows out. I want to stop and cry so bad, but I know that crying is not an option. I wasn't one to cry until my sister's disappearance. Even now I don't cry much, just a little more than I used to. And who wouldn't cry if your sibling was missing?

I'm now at forty-five and my arms are on fire. I have to grind my teeth together to keep from moaning over the pain. My back is tight and my breath is heavy. Finally I am done with my push-ups! I stand up and ask if I could please have some water. My dad nods, and I get to have a big gulp of heavenly, ice-cold water.

"Okay, now that you have had your little break, you must get back to work," he tells me. "You have done your bit of cardio on the treadmill, so now it is time to work on your muscles." He guides me to the pull-up bar.

"You will do pull-up ladders. You will start at a certain number like five, work up to fifteen, then work back down to five."

"Okay," I reply. I hop up on the pull-up bar, hanging my body, trying to stay in good form. I do five pull-ups, fast and easy. My dad lets me have a minute break, and then I am up on the pull-up bar again. Seven was easy, but after seven I start pushing it. I still make ten though.

My arms are sore and tired, but I know not to complain. I am up to fifteen, and ten seemed easy compared to this round. On eleven, my arms want to give out, but I stay strong and push myself through it. I finally make fifteen, but the last three pull-ups aren't in such great form. My dad does not say anything though.

Going down the ladder seems easy. My arms are now stiff and sore though; I bet I am going to feel it in the morning. My dad has me do tuck-ups to work my core, as well as sit-ups (three hundred of them), plank holds, ab crunches on the machine, and a lot of static holds. That isn't all though. He has me do all together two hundred push-ups but different types, such as diamonds and clap push-ups. He tells me that he wants me to use my body as a weight to get back into shape, and then I can lift.

I work out for three hours straight; I'm now dead and very hungry as well, but of course my dad has different ideas. He hands me this drink.

"What the heck is this?" I ask him.

"It's a protein drink. You need to drink it; it will help you build muscle and recover better," he says.

"I can't drink this; it looks like mixed-up dog poop!" I tell him.

"Oh, get over it. Just think of it as chocolate milk. The flavor is chocolate, so it can't taste that bad. Think about it… wouldn't you rather drink that and build muscle than eat three steaks at once and get sick?" he asks me.

"Um…I think I will eat three steaks," I say.

"Just drink it!" he tells me.

I take a sip, and actually, it doesn't taste that bad. My dad says that he mixed it with almond milk so it has less sugar. It just tastes like sugar-free chocolate milk, like they even have that, but, hey, I am being descriptive.

I take a shower and then eat a steak burger that my dad makes for me. He says I still need to eat a lot of meat for that protein. Meat is one of the best sources of protein, and it helps build muscle. It is also more natural than protein drinks, but he still is making me drink them.

Faith

I am so sore that I can barely walk. I have trouble just getting out of bed. Do you think that my dad cares though? No. He is making me work out again this morning. This time he is having me put on all of my snow clothes: hat, gloves, overalls, coat, snowshoes, everything! He is making me run in them outside—not just running in the field, no, he is having me run up and down a hill blanketed with a foot of snow. Joy! I am smart enough not to complain to his face though, because if I did, I would probably have to do push-ups out here in the snow or something.

My run is harder than I expected it to be. It is cold, my face feels frostbitten even though it isn't, I have to waddle up the hill because I weigh too much, and my nose keeps running. I am almost tempted to eat the snow so I can have some cold water because my dad "forgot" to bring out my water bottle. Then I see some yellow snow and figure I'm better off being dehydrated.

My run lasts twenty minutes and then I am done, well, with my cardio anyway. My dad at least allows me to stay inside and warm up for a bit until I have to work out again. My muscles are warm, but my face and fingers are frozen. My dad makes me some protein hot chocolate, which is his chocolate protein powder put in actual milk (surprise, surprise) and heated up in the microwave. It doesn't taste that bad, but I would prefer actual hot chocolate any day. After I finish, he makes me eat scrambled eggs with whole wheat, peanut butter toast. It is quite tasty and fills me up.

My dad takes me back down to the fitness room and makes me repeat all of my muscle workouts from yesterday. I don't do too well because my arms and abs are so sore. He seems a little bit nicer today, but he still gets after me over good form and pushing myself.

I am finally done with my workout, and again I have to drink another protein drink. For lunch I eat a grilled chicken sandwich with a cup of steamed vegetables and a side salad. Yum! I usually eat healthy, healthier than most. Ever since I was a young teen, I have always believed in working out and eating healthy. My whole family is like that.

I check Facebook to see if I have any more e-mails from Brian. Nope, none. He better be sticking to his plan. I decide that since I am in a decent mood today, other than feeling sore, I am going to clean my sister's room. I haven't been in her room since the day she went missing. I tell myself that it will make me feel better to go through her stuff and feel like she is still here. Sometimes I feel that I act like she is dead. She almost does seem dead to me though. I never hear her, see her, or talk to her anymore. When someone is gone for so long in a relationship, they can seem dead to a person. That is why most superstars get a divorce because they are never around each other. One is either off shooting a film, or the other is usually off on a concert tour, and they never see each other. So after a while they wonder if they even know each other anymore. They used to be so close, but when they find themselves living without that person, it is like the person is dead or out of their lives completely.

Of course I would never want Lily and me to lose our connection, not even on purpose. Though times get tough, like now, I wonder even if I have her back will it still be the same? Will it go back to the way it used to be? Or will our connection be stronger or just odd? I guess I won't personally know until I have her back.

I will admit that I am scared, but I will do what is best for her, and if I must save her, then sure as heck I am going to do it!

Going through her room is a hard task. Not only is it messy but seeing all of her valuable stuff also bothers me. I make her bed, put her clothes away, vacuum her floor, and dust. I cry a few times just seeing all of her stuff left here, like she is carrying on with a regular day until later that afternoon she is kidnapped against her will. People upset me so much. How can people think like that? Kidnap innocent kids just for money. How wrong.

As I am cleaning her room, I find a book peeking out from under her bed. It is the scrapbook that I made her for her birthday a year ago. I decide, since I am mostly done cleaning, that I will look through it. The front cover is a picture of Lily and me in Chicago. We are sitting on the rim of a fountain. My mom took a still picture of the water running and Lily and I laughing. The picture is remarkable. I flip through the pages. Most of them are of us on vacation, but there are some of us hanging out together at home. My favorite one is of us dressed up as gangsters for Halloween. Instead of P. Diddy she was P. Lily, and I was Mac Miller. That was my favorite Halloween costume ever!

The next picture I look at shows the day that has haunted me forever. We are standing on the balcony of our stairs; Lily, my friends, and I all took a picture together. I wanted just to hang out with my friends, and after that picture I told her to go do something else. My friends and I were planning to do our nails, and she wasn't invited. She got so mad that after my friends' pedicures, I walked to my room and realized the she had taken a Sharpie and wrote "Screw you" all over my new Coach purse. I was so mad that I ran out of my room and met her at the top of the stairs; she was coming up to use the bathroom. I was so mad that I grabbed her by the shoulders and shook her, yelling in her face, "How dare you! You no-good (bad words filled in the rest). I can't believe you!" While trying to push me off of her, she screamed in my face, "Well, maybe you shouldn't have been acting so selfish. I hate you!"

At that moment I had only one reaction, and I can never take it back. For some reason I felt the need to push her, and she tumbled backward. No, not on her butt but off our catwalk balcony. Seeing her body flip in the air, a step away from hurting herself, sickened me. My friends gasped. The second I pushed her I knew I had done something terrible. When she landed, she landed on our couch below, thank goodness. My friends and I ran down the stairs to see if she was all right. The whole time I was screaming, "Lily, I'm so sorry...I didn't mean to." As I reached her, I was going to pick her up, but she slapped me across the face. I felt a sudden crack, but it was not my jaw. No, it was my heart breaking.

"Don't touch me! Don't even come near me! How dare you! I hope you rot in hell!" she screamed to me—and I mean screamed! My friends were silent. She got up with a tear-streaked face and limped to the kitchen. I would have followed her, but I was too shocked to communicate. I was left there with the pain of what she just said. My family doesn't believe in wishing someone would go to hell unless they really mean it. Unless it is necessary, which it hardly ever is. So when those words came out of my sister's mouth, it was the worst thing I had ever heard.

It took us a day or two to finally communicate. She was okay, just had a hip out and a headache. After a week or so, we forgave each other, and we haven't had a fight that big since. So, now, looking back at that picture, it makes me realize that life isn't perfect. There will never be such a thing as "perfect" here on earth. There may be perfect in heaven but not on earth at this moment. It just shows that there will never be a perfect mom or dad, sister or brother, boyfriend or girlfriend, or even a best friend. Though there are days that we wish it were like that, we will never truly get our way. Just remember, even though you have a bad day one day doesn't mean that tomorrow won't be wonderful. Heck, it might be pretty darn amazing! But what you need to have…is faith.

The Whisper

I got the most wonderful news today. The station called us in, and the police have agreed to follow along with my plan! Isn't that amazing! We plan to start raising money to come up with the two million, even though the officers say that we could shortchange him a bit and he wouldn't know the difference. He is obviously not going to stand there and count the money while the person across from him (me) wants to punch him in the face so badly. They tell me that they will have a SWAT team nearby in hiding. We plan to have another meeting with them in two days.

A day later:

School started again today. I miss having the freedom of Christmas vacation, but at least I got to see West today! He met me by my locker this morning.

"Hey, how was your Christmas break?" he asks.

"It was okay. New York went pretty well, but spending a Christmas without my sister was pretty hard," I tell him.

"Yeah, I completely understand," he says.

Then he does something really weird. He puts his hands around my tiny waist and pulls me in close to him. I think he is going to kiss me, but instead he whispers in my ear, "Listen, I know it's hard for you to open up to a lot of people because most of them you can't trust, but I just want you to know that I am always here for you. If you ever need a friend to talk to, I'm here, and I will listen. Always."

He lets go of me and takes a step back. Shivers run up my spine; the feeling of his hands on my waist has left a warm spot. I wish they were still there. I know he pulled me in close just to whisper to me, so no one could hear, but it almost felt like more than just a whisper. It felt like he was holding me, keeping me safe. When I was in his grasp, I felt like nothing could hurt me, that I was finally loved and understood. What he said to me was like God's words coming from an angel's lips. I thrived on every word.

"Thank you, that means a lot," I say, almost in tears. Happy tears, knowing that more than one person is here for me. It means the world to me, especially coming from a man that I look up to.

He nods and then off he goes. I wish I could say something more, but the bell rings and it's time for me to head off to class as well.

Most of the classes drag on, only because it is hard getting back into the boring class schedule. My dad sends me a text at noon saying that I am not allowed to work out at the school tonight; I need to come home to work out instead. My first reaction is *great*, but I end up replying, "OK."

As I walk in the door, my father has just gotten home

from work. He is still in his suit and tie. He hands me a protein hot chocolate.

"You need something warm to drink before your workout; it's cold outside," he says.

"Oh, really? I didn't notice," I say sarcastically. It has been really cold for the last couple days but no snow. Not even on New Year's Eve or New Year's Day. It's only January but I wish it were July.

My workout consists of mostly cardio today. My dad tells me that my muscles need a day to recover. I wouldn't call his cardio a recovery though. He puts me on one of those spinners. It looks like a bike but stays in place while you pedal as fast as your legs can move. He has me spinning for a whole hour. Yeah, a whole hour! But he does give me a tiny break after my first thirty minutes. My legs are tired afterward, but that doesn't make him feel bad for me. He makes me do some plyometric exercises with leg squats, power jumps, and balance techniques. That only lasts a half hour though, and the last half hour I get to stretch.

I'm drenched in sweat from head to toe. I can barely walk or move my legs; my dad says it is because I have worked them to their max. I'd say! He makes me another protein drink, and for supper I have a taco with ground chicken, lettuce, tomatoes, salsa, green peppers, and a little bit of cheese. It is wrapped in a high-fiber, soft tortilla shell. My dad doesn't allow me to have any sour cream; he says it has too much fat. On the side he makes me brown rice. My mom has made me zucchini bread for dessert. I am only allowed one slice even though it is high in fiber.

I take a shower after supper and finish some homework.

I check Facebook and then look on the calendar. It is only January 4th, but I only have three and a half weeks until I rescue my sister.

Just as I am thinking how I can make two million dollars, my mom comes in.

"I have an idea," she says.

"Okay, what is it?" I ask.

"We won't be able to make two million dollars in close to four weeks, but we can make a good amount of money. What I am thinking we can do is start a running fund-raiser for the county where we run/walk to raise money," she explains.

"Mom, that's a great idea!" I tell her.

"I know. That's what I thought too," she says as she gives me a high five.

"So how do we set this whole thing up?" I ask her.

"Well, I will have to do some research and talk to the community center about it, but I will keep you informed. Okay?" she asks.

"Okay, sounds good!" I tell her and head off to bed.

I wake up not being able to move my legs. I am not paralyzed, I am just very sore. I take a Tylenol, which seems to help a bit. Then I have to get ready for school.

School is the same as it was yesterday, long and boring. West and I talk during study hall, but all we talk about is how my dad is trying to train me.

When I get home, I find a note on the counter from my dad stating what I need to eat for an after-school snack:

JAYLENE HALL

a peanut butter sandwich on wheat toast with one percent cottage cheese. The snack has a good percent of protein in it. When my dad gets home, he makes me do a workout video consisting of cardio and ab work. To tell you the truth, it isn't that easy. It lasts for an hour, and then he makes me do my pull-up and push-up exercises. Then for supper I eat a filet mignon that my mother grilled; it's delicious! I have steamed veggies to go with it.

I go to bed after I do my homework. I am truly tired.

My Running Buddy

It is finally Friday, and I am going to a movie with West, Chelsea, Brett, and Lena after school. It's finally nice to hang out with some friends for a change. My mom knows I am going.

The movie is great! As I pull into my driveway and walk inside, my dad is waiting for me. I'm thinking this can't be good.

"So instead of coming home and working out like you're supposed to, you ditch it and go party with your friends, eh?" he asks.

"Dad, I was not partying with my friends! We just went to a movie, so get off my case, okay?" I tell him. I can tell I've made him mad because now he is all up in my face. "No, I am not going to back off your *case!*" he yells. "You knew that you needed to come home and train! Training is way more important than your friends are."

"Dad, give me a break! I didn't know that I had to work-out *every* day. I need a rest once in a while."

"Well, I am your coach and I will tell you when you get

to have your break, but I was not planning on your break tonight! You listen to what I say and respect my decisions with no hesitation! Got me?" he screams.

At this point I am in tears. "I hear you!" I yell back. I run to my room and slam the door. It feels like all of this drama is starting all over again. I just lie on my bed as silent tears streak my face.

My dad shakes me awake, great! Now I am in our fitness room doing fifteen pull-ups. Joy. I have started to notice a little bit of chub disappearing from my midsection, and I have only been working out for about two weeks. It is because I am doing so much cardio. I am still muscular from gymnastics but not enough to my dad. He says after my second week he will have me start lifting weights, since he figures that I am already in good enough shape to get bulky. He is still cooking me healthy meals. I haven't eaten anything high in fat or sugar, except for yesterday when I had buttered popcorn at the movies.

After I finish my workout today, he tells me that tomorrow I will be down in his racecar shop lifting tires. I'm thinking, *what*? He tells me that I need to wear clothes to get dirty in. At least his shop is heated so I am not in the cold. At this point I think my dad has gone a little crazy.

The warm shower feels good against my sweaty skin. I feel and smell better. Chelsea and I decide to go shopping. I explain to her in the car about my plan of rescuing my sister. She is astounded. Of course whatever I tell Chelsea, she has to relate it to fashion somehow. She tells me that I should buy one of those spy outfits and wear it to my location spot so I look more professional when I rescue my sister. I laugh in her face, but she is serious. I tell her that I will think about it.

She finds this black leather jacket that has a black belt with a silver buckle wrapped around it. It looks like something a biker chick would wear but more fashionable and not as much Harley-Davidson style. She finds a pair of black leather pants to go with it. When I try them on they feel almost like a pair of skinny jeans but more, um, leathery? Ha-ha. Then you won't believe the shoes she has me try on! They are black leather, high-heeled boots. The leggings ride up to my knees. They look dangerous and sassy. She makes me try them on all together. If I wore this in the mall, I would be called "goth," but wearing it to the location would look fricking great! I look rough, but I look hot at the same time. Like I say, dangerous and sassy. Chelsea gives me no choice but to buy them. She can talk me into almost anything!

I lay the bags of my new merchandise on the shelf in my closet, and I change my clothes. I put on the oldest outfit I have. Apparently I have to go lift racecar tires. Let's see how this workout goes!

My dad has set up different obstacles for me to go through. One obstacle I have to do is run through tires in different patterns like football players do. Another one I have to do is different lifts, such as bicep curls and swimmer's press. I also have to do push-ups around a tire. There are other obstacles, but he makes me repeat them all three times! For the bonus at the end, he makes me carry two tires and run up a hill. It's harder than it looks! I can barely run; it's more like a skip. I look like a fail! The workout lasts two hours and I am exhausted, but of course he doesn't care. He makes me run three miles! I'm sick of this already!

Sunday comes and my dad finally lets me have a rest day—which isn't doing what ever I want to; it's sleeping. He makes me lie on the couch all day, watching TV, sleeping, and drinking a recovery formula. It consists of vitamins, minerals, and some protein to help my muscles recover faster. It tastes way better than the whey protein does! While I am helplessly bored on the couch, I am texting West. We don't talk about much. We don't really have a lot to say to each other. I'm not sure why though.

It is Monday. After school I have another meeting with the investigators. We decide that, instead of showing him the open cash, we will put one thousand dollars in each envelope inside the brief case. Only we won't fill all of the envelopes up with real money. We will stuff most of them with strips of paper the size of money, but they will be blank. We will only fill five envelopes with actual money. We are going to put ten one-hundred-dollar bills in each envelope. So in the end we will only be giving him five thousand dollars. We are hoping that he will not want to look through all of the envelopes, but if we leave the actual money envelopes on the top, we doubt he will want to check the bottom stacks.

My parents tell me that they are willing to lend the five thousand dollars but will not give it to me until the day before I set off to the location.

After our meeting I have to do my workout. I seem to have more energy to work out since my body is rested up. I have to do a cardio video and an abs video. It's not as hard as my dad's workouts, but it's not easy! He also makes me run an additional three miles today. As I am running, I feel my right hip pop out of place. It's kind of painful but I carry on with my run.

When I wake up, my hip really hurts. I complain to my mom, and she tells me that she will take me to the chiropractor after school. I can barely walk though. The nurse makes me wear an ice pack on my hip during school.

After visiting the chiropractor, he said that my hip was out, really out. It had been out for a while, but I didn't notice it until running triggered it. Dad still makes me workout though. I have to repeat the workout I started out with. I am able to do it faster since my body is used to the workout by now. My dad tries to switch up the workouts on me so I have muscle confusion. He says I am running out in the snow again tomorrow. Great!

I have started to see a difference in my mood. Since I have been working out, I feel like I have a lot more energy. It is also a way to release anger that's inside of me.

My dad actually gives me permission to bring a friend along running today. I choose West. Chelsea has to work. So after school West and I change into our snow clothes and head outside to my big hill. My dad knows West and his parents since he is one of the guys I hang out with a lot. My dad respects him; he says that he is "a good kid," which is true.

He makes us warm up and then sends us off to run a mile in the snow. I'm guessing Dad doesn't feel like coaching sprints today, so he chooses a long distance. He watches us closely as we run in my cornfield. If I run to the fence and back it would be close to two hundred meters, so I have to run to the fence and back eight times to make it a mile. West is good at keeping up since he is used to running in pads for football. We talk about his basketball practices and how he has basketball practice after our run.

West is really active and buff. I want to put my hands around his biceps so bad and ask him to flex, but that would be kind of weird. He tells me that I have good endurance and that I should do cross-country, but I tell him no. I tell him that I would rather do track than cross-country, even though I have never tried cross-country before.

We finish, and my dad tells us to meet him inside for some protein hot chocolate after we change out of our snow clothes. Well, let's just say we have a few minutes to spare so we tackle each other in the snow and throw snowballs at each other.

We go up to my garage to take off our overalls and coats. I have thick pajamas underneath my outfit, because to me wool pj's underneath my overalls keep me warmer. West has a Carhartt long-sleeved shirt under his overalls, with his sweatpants. After he takes off his coat he goes, "Darn, my shirt is soaked!" I kind of chuckle. Then he just throws his shirt off and leaves it hanging on the coat rack to dry.

Oh, my gosh! You want to talk about drop-dead gorgeous abs! His whole stomach is a boulder. I swear, you could chuck a brick at it and it would ricochet off. I can't help myself; I am just standing there like a dork staring at his abdomen. It's weird because it's not the first time I have seen him with his shirt off. I saw him at the pool last summer, and I see him working out in our school's gym without a shirt, but it's so weird. I think he has gotten more muscle and bulk; that's why it surprises me.

He catches me staring. "You okay?" he asks. I jump out of my daze. "Oh yeah, I'm fine. Uh…how much do you work out a day?" I ask him.

"Oh, it depends…we work out during basketball, which is about an hour, and then I go lift or run for another two. So I work out about three hours a day, maybe more," he says. Then he looks down at his own stomach and kind of laughs.

"Oh, I see…well, it definitely shows." I chuckle softly. He laughs a little and then we go inside. He throws on an extra Under Armour sweatshirt before he walks in.

He likes the protein hot chocolate. I tell him that this is the only hot chocolate my dad will let me drink. Then he has to leave for basketball. I escort him outside to his car. I thank him for running with me. He says, "No problem, call me up anytime you need a running partner."

I smile. Then he kind of gently puts his hands on my face and slowly pulls me in. He's finally going to kiss me.

"Um…hey, West?" my mom yells from the door. Ruined. He has to pull away before our lips can even meet. I can tell he is a bit embarrassed.

"Uh…yes, Tamra?" he asks.

"Don't forget your snow clothes in our garage, sweetie," she says with a smile. My mom can be really sweet to people, but this just wanted to make me sick. I mean of all times, did she *really* have to butt in with her sweet tone when I was just about to kiss a really hot guy? I mean, come on!

"Oh, thanks," he says nicely. Then he goes to get his stuff in the garage. I kind of stand there feeling a little stupid. I don't really know what to say like, "Can we try this again?" or "Sorry my mom butted in on our *almost* first kiss." I mean really, what was I supposed to say? So instead I just stand there looking stupefied. I think he kind of feels the same way, because when he comes back, he says a good-bye and then kind of hesitates before pulling me in for a hug. It is weird because the hug is like one that you get from a person you know, but you can't remember the name. Yeah, it is that type of hug. So my first kiss with West is totally ruined, but, oh well... I'm sure he will try to pop the move again sometime.

Stress

Today I am sore, no surprise. Apparently West made me run a little harder than usual yesterday. For some reason something is bothering me. I am not feeling right, and I feel a need to be angry. I only have two weeks until I meet Brian at the location. I think about Lily; I think about her all the time. It sickens me to know that she is in someone else's hands.

I cannot keep anything down today. After eating my mom's stew, I had to run to the toilet and puke it up, not on purpose though. My mom keeps telling me that I cry in my sleep at night. My workout is hard today too. I cannot do the last five reps of anything; my body gives out or maybe it's my mind giving up on itself. Part of me says, OK, you've had enough. The other part of me says push harder, do it for her!

The next day is not any better. I have to stay home from school. I'm too sick. I puke my guts out all day, and I cannot sleep at night. My dad tells me to rest, drink my recovery formula, and keep good hygiene. My mom insists that she take me to the doctor; sure enough, his answer is stress. "You are stressing your body out and not just from working out, but emotionally. That is what's causing you to vomit; you get so worked up that after you eat your stomach gets upset."

I know he is right. I am nervous; my life is on the line and so is Lily's. I have to save her, I just have to. The rest of the week I stay home. I'm way behind on my schoolwork and my grades are falling. I am a mess...again. It's like I am starting back at the beginning. My dad still makes me workout, just not as hard. It mostly consists of cardio to keep the fat off.

I can't sleep either. I sit up in bed and think about everything that could happen at the location. What if I get shot? What if she gets shot? I can't see the sister I have been missing for four months get shot before my eyes. That thought sends bitter chills up my spine. Then I get angry at the world. I get angry at the evil people who live in it. How much people infuriate me, but I have to let it go. God knows that she and I are the strong ones in this situation.

On Monday I am feeling better; I only have four days left. My dad makes me target practice with his shotguns and handguns. I used to go hunting with him before I started high school. I knew a lot about guns, the dangers of them, and the excitement after you shoot a big buck. He is making me take a handgun to the location. He says that even though I am breaking the rules, it is only for my safety. I agree with him. He gives me a pep talk about when I should use it and when I should not. That gets me nervous. I don't want to think about using the gun for protection, but I know there is a big risk of it happening. I go to school, and then I have a meeting with my lawyer. I have a court hearing for Sabrina Hope on the day after the rescue. It will be in New York, so that will be easy to attend since I will already be in New York.

I start packing on Tuesday. I pack the clothes Chelsea bought me and everything else that I could possibly need. I make sure all of my homework is done, and I say good-bye to all my friends.

Wednesday is the day. I am boarding my flight. It is five in the morning, and I'm not just traveling on an average plane, I am flying on a private jet. The government has sent me out to New York with bodyguards and undercover policemen. My family is at my side. I am so nervous that I puke again before we land. My parents are trying to keep me calm, but it's not helping. The bodyguards lead us into our hotel and tell us to stay in the hotel room until told. They don't want Brian or Frappiero finding us out in public. They could be searching for me, and I could be in real danger. I pray to God that he keeps my whole family safe as I sit, a nervous wreck, in my hotel room.

Officially Ready

I am officially scared. I had a rampage earlier this morning for it is Thursday, and my heart is becoming ill. I am not allowed out of the room, but I didn't care. I wanted breakfast and I was not waiting for them to deliver it. I was getting the breakfast buffet down in the lobby. As I was waiting in line, no one seemed to notice me. All of a sudden a man just cut in front of me in line. He knew I saw him, so instead of confronting him, I made a big scene. I was angered, not only at him but at the way people are so selfish. I hit the plate right out of his hands, and it hit the floor with a loud crack. Everyone turned and stared. I had a muscle shirt on with yoga pants, it looked like I just walked out of bed, but you could see every muscle toned and bulging out of my body. Going on six weeks of training like a sergeant, no one could last.

The man turned around, suddenly scared after looking at my face, then my biceps. "Miss...I'm sorry," he said with a shy voice.

"Sorry? I want food just as much as you do, and you think

it's right to just walk in front of me when I have been waiting here longer than you have been waiting on your mom to whip your…" I heard someone fake a cough as if to say, "Don't say the 'a' word!"

I did not finish the sentence, but I still stayed all up in his face. "Listen, when you respect other people, they will respect you," I told him, and then I walked away. Everybody was still staring at me as I walked out of the lobby, but I didn't care. My mom met me in the doorway.

"Are you stupid? What in the name are you doing here?" she asked, frightened and shocked.

"Let's go to the room," I said.

"You know you aren't supposed to leave!" she told me. "You could be in danger!"

"Oh mom…shut up!" I yelled at her. "You guys are so worried about me being in danger right now, but what about tomorrow? I'll be coming face-to-face with the monster who ruined Lily's and our lives! He could kill me, Mom! He could…kill me…" I started to cry. She let me lie in her arms limp and cry. My tears soaked her sleeve, and my heavy weight leaned against her, but for once she was a mom. For once in a long time, she held me, loved me, wiped my tears away, and told me that it would be okay.

I know she is right…I will be okay.

Back in the room, I clean my act up. I have to be strong. There is no way that I can have a nervous breakdown tomorrow at the location. I unpack my clothes for tomorrow and my map. I am trying to occupy myself. Nothing is helping. I am pacing back and forth, and I am writing things in my notes about how it will be when my sister is finally home with me again. I brush my teeth and hair. I have to do anything to keep my mind off of tomorrow.

West calls me. He tells me that he is flying into New York tomorrow morning so he can see me after the rescue. He wants to make sure that I'm okay. He says that he is also bringing Chelsea and her boyfriend along with him. He tells me to be strong, and the weird thing is, right before he hangs up, he says that he loves me.

After hearing him say that, I start to softly cry…happy tears. I say "I love you" back. I know that with West on my side, I will make it. I will make it out alive and with my beautiful sister.

I lie stiffly in my bed, not able to sleep. Gut feelings of horrible thoughts rush through my head. My heart is racing so fast that it is almost hard to breathe. I try to take deep breaths, but nothing is helping. I am sincerely a mess. I keep looking at the clock; I finally go to sleep at 3:00 a.m. My body is too tired to stay up another minute. I have a nightmare of me chasing someone and falling. I don't remember anything else, but when I wake up, I see the light of dawn.

I order breakfast, but I do not eat. I can't stand to even play with my food without getting nauseated. My parents try to persuade me, but I don't listen.

During the afternoon I have to sit through another meeting in our little hotel room. We go over the signals, the timing, the money situation, and protection. They make me take an addition two-hour nap, so I am rested up in time for action.

At three o'clock they make me get dressed. I wear the outfit that Chelsea told me to wear, but instead of the high-heeled boots, I wear black Pumas. They are way more comfortable than the boots. Also, who would want to run in boots?

I am shivering from head to toe. My nerves are all out of whack. They hand me my prized possession: the briefcase. It only has five thousand dollars in it; the rest are shreds of paper. My dad, off to the side, hands me his handgun, which I slip in my back pocket. He tells me that I should not shoot anyone unless needed. He also tells me that if I have to shoot someone, I will have to live with it the rest of my life. I could not do that…he says that he couldn't either. He starts to cry.

In my eighteen years of life, never once have I seen my dad cry over me. I have seen him cry over my sister and her disappearance, but never once has he cried about me. It breaks my heart. I pull him in for a hug as he sobs on my shoulder. "Dad, it will be okay. I will be okay," I reassure him.

It seems to make him feel better. He tells me that he loves me and to be careful.

My mom is having a breakdown. She just keeps repeating, "Just get you both out alive." I keep telling her to breathe. She is so nervous.

Finally some undercover people usher me out. I am to take a taxi like a normal person to the location, only an undercover policeman will be driving.

I kiss my family good-bye and then hop into the taxi. My heart is pounding out of my chest, but I am ready. I am ready to bring her home, hold her, kiss her soft cheeks, and tell her that I love her again.

You

I look up at the building. It is five o'clock on the dot. My blood is running through my veins like wildfire. My heart is beating as fast as a racehorse.

I step out of the taxi and give a nod to the taxi driver (aka "undercover policeman"). I already know that there is a SWAT team in hiding. I walk up to the old double doors. The date is initialed above it. I am at the right place. I creak open the doors, putting my hand on my back pocket. It is pitch dark with only a little light showing through the broken windows on the other side of the hallway.

I take one step and the floor creaks. I stop, waiting to hear a noise. I think my heart stops as well. I keep slowly tiptoeing down the hallway. I am not sure if I should yell a hello or find them first. I go with my instinct.

I walk down to the end of the hall. At least I can see down here with the windows. I see an open door to the side, the only door that is still attached to its hinges. I walk through it. I have my flashlight on now, and my senses are sharp. I stop only to hear a sudden noise, a creak above me. I shine my flashlight up toward the ceiling to see if someone is above me or if the ceiling is falling through. Nothing is above me, so someone has to be upstairs, but how do I find the flight of stairs? I start to worry. I am about to panic, but I tell myself to breathe.

I walk slowly around the corner to another hallway. There, around the corner, is a flight of stairs. I am wary that they might fall through. I have to take a risk though. I walk up two steps at a time; that way there isn't as much pressure on each and every board. They are loud, and I start to feel like I am being watched. I look below me. No one. I look ahead of me. No one. I keep stepping up until I reach the landing. My feet and hands are trembling. I am silent.

As I am standing there, still as can be, I hear a creak and then a door open. I'm about to pee my pants. I have to hold my hand over my mouth to keep from screaming. Then…I hear it. I hear the voice of a chilling stranger who I will soon know so well.

"I see that you haven't backed out, eh?" Brian's chilling voice rings through the hallway.

I uncover my mouth. "I wouldn't back out…you have my sister, you creep, not some rag doll!" I tell him. I regret saying it, thinking that he might hurt me, but at this point I am too angry.

This creep has held my sister hostage for four months now. He watches her every move, savors her every word, and rules over her. He is sick to me, and he knows it.

"Where's the money?" he asks as he steps forward, closer.

"I want to see you in the light first," I reply. I follow him down to the lightened part of another hallway.

His face shocks me. He is not wearing a mask. He has blackish hair and brown eyes. He looks messy and dirty. He has on ragged clothes and smells like vodka. I want to puke. He looks a bit different from his Facebook pictures.

"Here's your money," I say as I slowly hand the briefcase to him but pull away before he can clutch it. "You're not here alone, are you," I confront him. He looks taken back. "It's just your sister and me, now hand it over!"

"No, where is she?" I start to yell. "I will give you the money…once I know she is here!"

He makes one sudden move. He takes his left arm and shoves me in the chest and then takes his right arm and grabs the briefcase. It happens so fast that I'm clueless about what to do. I take off after him. I'm so glad my dad had me doing cardio exercises and endurance. I am able to catch up to him like lightning. I am able to get my arm wrapped around his neck in a chokehold. With the other arm, I grab back the briefcase. I then kick him to the floor. He pulls my legs out from under me and begins to almost choke me, but I don't let him get that far. I swing my fist across his face and then jab him right in the nose. I hear a crack from his face, and he lets go of my throat. I slide out from under his hold, and I start running for another flight of stairs. I am guessing that the building has at least five floors.

As I am running up the stairs, he gains power and grabs my ankles. My body falls with a hard thump against the stairs. My chest feels solid, and I get the wind taken out of me. He starts to drag me down the stairs.

I am able to flip my body around and kick him. He falls the rest of the way down, but that doesn't stop him. As I try to run up the stairs again, he comes up fast enough and grabs my head, thrusting me backward. We both fall down the stairs together, and as we are falling, a board breaks loose. My right ankle falls through the board and I am stuck. I can feel splinters piercing my skin around my ankle. He is again coming at me.

I am able to do only one thing. I pull my ankle as hard as I can out of the broken board. I instantly feel my ankle go cold. I feel blood trickling down. It's burning, but I ignore it. I plunge toward him; again both of us fall down the stairs, piling up at the bottom. He acts like he is knocked out, but I think he is faking it. I sit on top of him with my gun pointed to the temple of his head.

"You made my life hell!" I tell him through clinched teeth. "You made my family suffer and live life like we had nothing! You took everything away from us! You took a person away that we loved so dearly!"

I see him open his eyes and stare at me. "I want to know where she is, otherwise I will put a bullet right into your sickening head!" I scream. After the words come out, I feel ashamed. I should have never told him that, nor should I tell anyone that. I am not like that. It's not me. I let my anger get the best of me, and I shouldn't have.

"I want the money..." he mumbles. I know it's time. I pull down the gun and put it back in my pocket while with my other arm, I am still barely chocking him. I punch him in the face until he is knocked out. I can't kill him...I wouldn't nor couldn't do it.

I start running up the stairs this time, screaming her name. "Lily! Lily! Oh, Lily, please answer me!" I start to cry as I am screaming.

I keep wandering down the dark hallways. They all have mice and rats running this way and that. It smells horrible, and you can hear birds fluttering on the third floor. My ankle hurts so bad that I begin to limp. I feel like I am going to die. My chest, ribs, and shins feel bruised. I just want to find her; that's all I want to do. I pray to the dear Lord that I will find her…and that we will be safe.

He must have answered my prayer because I hear a scream, a girl's scream. It sounds like it is in a room a little farther down the hall. I scream her name again, "Lily!" Again she replies with a scream. I start sprinting to where I hear the scream. I end up down the hall by a door that is closed. I bang on it and try to open it, but it is locked. The screaming gets louder on the other side of the door.

"Just wait, Lily! I'm coming! Hold on, baby!" I yell to her. The door will not open. I decide to back away from it while I still have room, then I run for it. I pound the door with my shoulder, pushing all my weight into it. I fall back, hard. It feels like I just broke every bone in my body, but with my extra strength, I do it again. I run for it, this time with all of my muscles flexed and ready for a pounding. I put so much force into it that it bangs open with a huge crash. The room is dark, and as soon as I run in, I feel someone grab me by my neck and pull me into his big body, holding me in a choke-hold. I am gasping for air.

I am able to elbow the person in the ribs, turn around, and kick the person square in the gut. I am able to make shadows out now since my eyes are adjusting to the darkness. I punch the person in the face, and then I get grabbed from behind. Another person tries to strangle me, but I am able to pull my gun out and fire it. I hear a scream of pain, and then I begin to get up until I hear another gun fire. My heart stops beating. I feel the worst pain in my life. My ankle, the same I ankle I cut, is now burning with rage. The man who I punched in the face has shot me in the ankle.

I am able to get up on my good leg and throw the gun out of his hand, punching him again. He falls back. I am happy to know that all of the working out has paid off. I take out my flashlight and turn it on. I still hear the slightest screaming in front of me. I shine the flashlight in front of me. There sits the person I almost died for. There sits the person I have missed for so long. There sits the girl that I have been wanting so badly. I run up to her; she is duct-taped to a wooden chair. I undo the tape quickly and pick her up. No one else except us and the beat-up guys (who are knocked out) are in the room. I throw her over my shoulders and run down the hallway. I run as fast as my bad ankle will let me. It's painful and I can barely pick it up, but I push through it.

I cannot run down the stairs, so we have to drag our butts down them as fast as we can. As soon as we reach the second floor, I yell into my hidden walkie-talkie, "Now!"

As soon as I say it, Lily and I keep running, but I hear people running through the doors downstairs.

I yell for them as we reach the top of the other set of stairs to get to the main floor where they are.

The SWAT team rushes over to us. A group of them pick us up and carry us out, while the others run upstairs to find Brian and the rest.

Finally

I am carried through the big doors with my sister in another guy's arms beside me. As we step outside, I see the light and I am blind for a few seconds. When I open my eyes, I am sitting down beside my sister. People are crowding around us from every direction. More people start to gather, and soon I know why. I have people hugging my sister and me, kissing us, and crying over us. My mom and dad are holding my sister so tightly. I look over at her, and she looks back at me. My heart is bursting. Her eyes are now a reality. She is back into physical form. I push my mom and dad and the rest of the people away from her. I hold her and she holds me. I start to bawl in her arms. She is crying mercy on me. I fall to my knees, and I pull her down with me. She hugs me so tight and so dear. I don't want to let go of her; I don't want to lose her again.

Finally I can hold her. Finally I can kiss her delicate cheeks. Finally I can stroke her hair, tell her that I love her, and see her every morning when I wake up. Finally.

My mom and dad collapse over us, hugging us, and

weeping over us. There are people surrounding us—family members, friends, and even strangers. They are all weeping with joy. As I let go of her gently, I put my hands together and start to pray.

"Dear Lord, you let me live. You gave her back to me. After all the suffering I went through, you still died for us on the cross, and I was going to die for my sister. Thank you!" I pray to him.

Everybody else is doing the same. They are all bowing their heads and getting on their knees. What a thing to see. I again hold my sister and kiss her forehead. My parents are falling apart. My mom gave birth to that child twelve years ago, and someone took her blessing away from her for four whole months. My mother did not know where her own daughter was for four whole months! The days that she bathed her, sang to her, played with her, laughed with her, and held her were all taken out of her hands.

We live in a cruel world. Life will never be fair. It's up to us to stay strong and know that there will always be better days. No matter how bad life may seem, as long as you pray to him for help, he will always listen.

The rest of the SWAT team moves us through the crowd. We are put on a helicopter hovering a few feet above the ground to be flown to the nearest hospital. They have to lift me up into it since my whole body has become weak under my ankle.

My parents, Lily, and I all sit in there with the pilot behind the gears. I turn to Lily, who is sitting next to me, and say, "I love you."

She kisses my cheek. "You saved me."

We arrive at the hospital and are taken into the emergency room. They have to remove the bullet from my ankle, pull the moved muscles back together, and sew it up. I can't walk on it for a while so I have to be in a wheelchair or on crutches, but I am to weak to walk so I choose the wheelchair.

Lily is fine but just really skinny. They want to make sure that she eats a lot. We have to stay the night in the hospital, but I don't want to move anyway. Her bed is right across from mine, and we have family members visiting all the time.

West, Chelsea, and her boyfriend come in right before the visiting hours are over. West sits beside my bed and holds my hand. Lily is asleep for now she can rest peacefully. After they gave her a bath, it relaxed her. West looks at her with tears in his eyes, and then he looks back at me. "You did it," he says; he leans in and kisses me. His soft lips feel so good against mine. My parents are right there watching us, but we don't care.

He pulls away after a while and begins to stroke my hair while Chelsea is lying beside me in my bed. Her boyfriend, Blake, is quiet in the corner. Somehow she and I both seem to fit in the small hospital bed. She tells me about their long flight and how happy she is that I'm alive.

I don't want to talk about what happened at the location; I just want to rest. As soon as they leave, I fall asleep.

I am now able to sleep knowing that I have my sister and family beside me safe and sound. Who would want anything better than that?

Sister Strong

Sitting in the tattoo parlor, I am going over what I want my tattoo to look like with the lady. It has been a month since the rescue, and my family is as happy as ever. After the court hearing the day after the rescue, Sabrina Hope is now free from her past. Well, she is free from her past in court, that is. While on the plane home, I decided that I wanted to get a tattoo where my scar is from the gunshot wound and the deep cut.

I tell the lady that I would like "Sister Strong" written across my scar, covering it. I would then like to have a cross for the "t" in "sister" and "strong." I want the color of the letters to be black and in cursive.

My parents are allowing this since I am eighteen, and it will be known as my battle scar.

The lady asks me, "Why do you want it to say 'Sister Strong'?"

"Oh, it means a great friendship between two sisters… like one would do anything for the other," I reply.

"Oh," she says in a seemingly confused voice.

"Have you ever tried to save your sister's life?" I ask.

She looks at me dumbly. "Uh…no?" she replies.

"That's what I thought," I say as I chuckle to myself.

The tattoo looks great, better than what I had anticipated. My sister is very impressed with it as well.

My sister and I now enjoy ourselves by going shopping together, talking about everything together, and having a good time together. We are almost back to normal for once. My mom is more relaxed, and my dad is home more. They are making their marriage work.

I am getting ready for track season. My ankle still hurts every now and then, but my coach says it will be good to exercise it. It's weird being with all my friends again and actually being more sociable. It's a lot easier, though, when you don't have all that stress on your shoulders. I feel like I am actually able to breathe again. Before it felt like everybody around me, including myself, was suffocating me. Now I feel happy and willing.

I was interviewed on the news all around the country. For one, after the SWAT team was able to arrest Brian and the rest, it was also able to find all of the missing children they had kidnapped in another abandoned building down the road. So not only did I save my sister, but I saved somebody else's son or daughter. They ended up rescuing seven other children. I feel very proud. They found the briefcase in the building where I left it to rescue Lily on the third floor. My parents let me keep the money that they had lent me.

I put the five thousand dollars in my savings for college. I have started to write songs more, and I want to go to the fine arts college in Chicago. My sister, on the other hand, wants to go to the Olympics for swimming.

After coming back to her real home, she has been able to talk about how she was treated and how bad it was. She was not beaten, but she was hardly fed or bathed. She says that it was the worst thing in her life, not knowing if she would ever see her family again.

Lily has been able to go back to swimming and is doing sports in the summer. She says that she will miss me this summer when I go off to college; I promise her that she can spend some weekends with me. She was super excited to hear that.

West and I became an "official" couple a few weeks after I was home and back in school. He insisted that he would take Lily and me out to the fanciest restaurant in Des Moines. So Lily got to be a part of our dinner date; she felt like a proud sister.

We are worried about how our relationship will last through college. West is going to play basketball in another state, while I am off to Chicago to dance and sing. He insists that we just try to date through college and see how it goes. I agree with him, and if it doesn't work out, it doesn't work out.

My track season ended great! I didn't do the best like most years; with my ankle I could only do sprints and not long distance. I still enjoyed it a lot, and my sister was at almost every meet cheering me on.

I still pray to God every day for bringing her back into my life; it was a real blessing. It has now made our relationship stronger. It even made my parents' relationship stronger! She is also so thankful that she was brought home safe; she refers to it as a second chance at life. Every time I see her sleep, I cry. Seeing her precious body now relaxed and in front of me makes me feel proud. I saved my sister. She saved me. From all the times I wanted to give up or quit working out or draw away from my loved ones, she stayed in my head pushing me forward. She kept me strong, and I love her for that.

On graduation day she sits there with her eyes full of tears, those big blue eyes all watery. She holds the most beautiful flowers in her hands and carries the most beautiful smile on her face. I know now that I am probably the best sister in the world; I am her best friend.

After getting my diploma, we hug tightly. She cannot hold back tears and neither can I. For so long I fought through blood and fire to find her and to find myself. Every part of me has been broken, torn, and put back together. Packing up my stuff is hard.

"Do you have to leave me?" she asks as I am taking everything out of my closet.

"No, honey, I won't ever leave you! I will always be in your heart. Right now I just have to go and live on my own, to fulfill another goal in my life and to become even more of who I want to be," I tell her.

"You don't have to be anything else to me. You are my hero, and that's all that matters. You don't have to be rich, famous, beautiful, or smart; I love you for who you are." she says as she hugs me.

"I love you too, but someday after my career has settled, I will have kids of my own so they can have brothers and sisters. Then I will tell them the story about you and me," I tell her. She understands.

"We are sister strong!" she says.

"Yes…yes we are," I say.

Epilogue

Looking forward twenty years later:

After graduation Macy attended the Columbia College of Chicago for fine arts in 2012. During her first year, she and West dated for three months but had to break up. They felt that the long-distance relationship wasn't working for them. She met another boy named Jacobson, two months after the breakup, in the city. They dated throughout her college years. She attended college for four years and got her bachelor's degree in dance, music, musical theater, and photography. After college she hit a recording studio and wrote a couple songs that hit number one on the charts. She toured around the world singing pop, known as a pop star. She also landed some parts in films and received an Oscar award for best actress in a movie she starred in. She was well known around the world and later wrote a book based on Lily and her. Lily toured a lot with Macy during her teen years and a lot of times would appear on stage at one of Macy's concerts.

Macy and Jacobson ended up getting married three years

later after they both graduated from college. Jacobson became a personal trainer in fitness and worked with Macy and others for better health. He toured with Macy a lot and was her workout buddy/coach. A year after being married, they built a huge house together and had three kids: May, Hope, and Trey.

Lily qualified for the Olympics in 2016 just after she turned sixteen. She was competing in track instead of swimming. After winning numerous times at the state championships in junior high and high school, she knew that track was for her. She brought home a gold in the one-hundred-meter dash and a silver in the two-hundred-meter dash. The next two years she was qualified into the Olympics, bringing home numerous golds and silvers. After retiring from track, Lily studied sports medicine. She then trained track athletes who wanted to try out for the Olympics. She didn't marry until she was thirty-one, and she had two daughters, who were only a year and a half apart, named Katrina and Lacey. Her husband was a doctor and his name was Kane.

Lily and Macy still stayed close throughout their lives. They were there for each other through thick and thin. They both were hard workers and exceeded in their work and family ethic. Their families were strong Christians.

See how much their relationship has changed since the beginning of the story?

You never know what you have until it's gone. Love, for example. If you go around asking people what love means, they will probably say it's something you want forever or something you never want to let go of. If you ask them what the most important things they love in life are, it will probably be God, family, and friends.

Most people can't imagine their life without their family, or some just want a family. We all know, though we don't want to think about it, that things can happen in one second. In a blink of an eye, in a matter of time, bad things happen and we don't understand why. Why was it put on us to carry on with this pain?

My sister and I were best friends. Sometimes we didn't seem like it; other times you couldn't split us apart. She was such a big part in my life, such a big part no one could actually understand. I remember when I wanted a baby brother or sister so bad that I actually begged my parents for one. I remember the exact day my mom told me she was pregnant and the exact day she gave birth to her.

As my sister got older, I got to see her life play out. I wanted to run home after school to play with her when I was younger. Seeing her infant body made me think of a real-life baby doll. I wanted to dress her, feed her, and play with her. We were six years apart; I couldn't do much with her until she got older.

As the years went by, things changed. We both got really busy, and we didn't see much of each other. It was my senior year, and she was only in sixth grade. I was to busy working out, practicing gymnastics, or hanging with my friends. She was the same way, so I only got to see her maybe every other day in the morning or at gymnastics practice. I did see her when we all ate supper together, but that didn't happen much because I just wanted to get fast food after sports practice.

She kept her focus on gymnastics, racing go-carts, and swimming. She was a great gymnast and traveled on the team with me, but she also could race a car at one hundred miles an hour and swim like a beast. I tried to come to most of her meets, but I did not make all of them. She sure made me proud though, and I could have never asked for a better sister.

Afterword

Most of you may know that this story did not really happen to my sister and me, though it has a great meaning to it. I wrote this so people could stop and think about the world we live in. Sometimes we are so caught up in ourselves that we forget our loved ones. I want people to know that with faith you can do anything. If you pray to him, sooner or later he will help you out. Remember that there are always better days, and live every day like it's your last. We are all human beings, and we aren't perfect. We make mistakes, but it's our job to learn from them.

I try my best to tell my sister how much I love her. Though I am busy like every other teen, I still always find time to tell her that I love her. I may not play dolls with her much or hang out with her much, but I always tell her that I love her. Those three words, "I love you," can change some-one's whole personality. As long as the person really means it, it can even change the world.

I know that you are not old enough to read this yet, my dear sister. I hope when you do, though, that you treasure it. I want you to read it when you are down or sad so it may cheer you up, because you know that your family loves you dearly.

I want you to read it when I am at college, so you remember that I am always here for you even if I am far away. I want you to also remember that I am always here if you ever need me. This world can be cruel, and everybody deserves a shoulder to cry on once in a while. I know that when you are older, you will do the most magnificent things! Don't let anybody change your bubbly attitude or make you feel like you aren't good enough, because you are. Always keep pushing hard to achieve your goals and never let people get in your way. You mean the world to me, remember that. I love you, Janae.

I hope other brother and sisters read this and realize how lucky they are. Even though brothers and sisters can get on our nerves sometimes, they still are God's creation. God blessed them into our world for a reason and we should acknowledge that.

———— ·◦·———

We know love by this, that he laid down his life for us, and we ought to lay down our lives for one another. How does God's love abide in anyone who has the world's goods and sees a brother or sister in need and yet refuses help?

Little children, let us love, not in word or speech, but in truth and action. And by this we will know that we are from the truth and will reassure our hearts before him whenever our hearts condemn us; for God is greater than our hearts, and he knows everything. Beloved, if our hearts do not condemn us, we have boldness before God; and we receive from him whatever we ask, because we obey his commandments and do what pleases him.

1 John 3:16-22

CPSIA information can be obtained at www.ICGtesting.com
Printed in the USA
LVOW131351280613

340697LV00001B/209/P

9 781478 709626